TWO
DUMB JOCKS

JEFF ERNO

Dreamspinner Press

Published by
DREAMSPINNER PRESS

5032 Capital Circle SW, Suite 2, PMB# 279, Tallahassee, FL 32305-7886 USA
http://www.dreamspinnerpress.com/

Two Dumb Jocks
© 2014 Jeff Erno.

Cover Art
© 2014 Paul Richmond.
http://www.paulrichmondstudio.com
Cover content is for illustrative purposes only and any person depicted on the cover is a model.

ISBN: 978-1-62798-967-1
Digital ISBN: 978-1-62798-968-8
Library of Congress Control Number: 2014940020
First Edition July 2014

Printed in the United States of America
∞
This paper meets the requirements of
ANSI/NISO Z39.48-1992 (Permanence of Paper).

Readers love the DUMB JOCK series by Jeff Erno

Dumb Jock

"The reader really does join Jeff's journey and rides along, the pace is realistic…. Recommended for a reader who wants to patiently retrace a coming out story and enjoys dipping back into the 80s."

—Hearts on Fire

"While it may not be believable to everyone, it was to me and I can honestly say I would recommend *Dumb Jock* to everyone who loves the nerd/jock trope"

—Greedy Bug Book Reviews

Another Dumb Jock

"*Another Dumb Jock* is an easy book to recommend. You will fall in love with the characters and enjoy watching two seemingly opposite people form a very special relationship. Highly Recommended!"

—Top 2 Bottom Reviews

Appearances Matter

"*Appearances Matter* by Jeff Erno is a great addition to the Dumb Jock series. I loved the portrayal of the characters, the exposition of bullying in schools, and the image of a popular jock seeing a wrong and righting it."

—Spectrum Books

Dumb Jock: The Musical

"What I loved most about this book was that for every negative, there was a positive. If you are a fan of *Glee* and *High School Musical*, I think you'll really enjoy this book."

—MM Good Book Reviews

By JEFF ERNO

Choosing America's Next Superstar
The Left-Hand Path
Trust Me
We Danced

DUMB JOCK SERIES
Dumb Jock
Another Dumb Jock
Appearances Matter
Dumb Jock: The Musical
Two Dumb Jocks

Published by DREAMSPINNER PRESS
http://www.dreamspinnerpress.com

— INTRODUCTION —

"TENNIS? YOU can't be serious."

Trevor scowled at him. "Put up or shut up, jock boy."

Bryan laughed. "Uh, okay, but it's not gonna prove anything. Tennis ain't even a real sport. It's like golf—even girls play it."

"Last time I checked, girls play basketball too. And ya better not let Dad hear ya dissin' golf."

Trevor referred to Jeff and Brett as his parents even though he wasn't really their kid. He was their son Adam's boyfriend and had been accepted as a member of the family. Bryan, too, was already beginning to feel similarly about them. He had immediately hit it off with both Adam and Trevor, but he still felt a bit awkward. He was the only member of the "family" who didn't play tennis. Brett's passions were golf and football, and Adam was into baseball, but as a family, their only shared athletic interest was tennis.

Trevor had taken him to the sporting goods store, and they were picking out his new racket. Bryan didn't want to sound like a complete dummy, but he honestly had no idea what he was doing.

When Bryan arrived in Florida, he instantly felt as if the loving and accepting environment he'd stepped into was paradise. He was embraced and encouraged by every member of the family, and within days he felt right at home. But he still battled with his inner demons. He still had days when he hated himself and wished he'd never been born.

"Distortions," Jeff had explained. "You have negative core beliefs, and you've got to root them out. Identify them and challenge them."

"But how?"

"Well, for example, when you think, 'My life sucks,' you have to tell yourself it's not true. Sit down and make a list of all the things in your life that don't suck. You'll see that many times it's just a matter of looking at the glass as being half full."

"I wish it were that easy," he confessed.

"No, depression's not easy, and people who trivialize it are speaking out of ignorance. But you're strong, Bryan. And you've got a lot of support. We all love you and know you're an amazing guy. We just gotta get you to see yourself the way *we* see you."

For the most part, Bryan was pretty upbeat. He didn't wallow around in self-pity, and he did a fairly good job of concealing the occasional low mood he did experience. Antidepressants also helped. He played on the university basketball team and had a full academic schedule. That didn't leave him a whole lot of time to feel sorry for himself.

He really didn't want to have the negative thoughts. He didn't want to feel blue, and he was making every effort to treat his depressive condition as an illness. That was how Jeff had explained it, and the doctor said the same thing. He wasn't crazy; he just had a medical condition, and it wasn't uncommon. Being in the environment he was in, he knew he was getting the help he needed to get better.

"Have you played before?" Trevor asked.

"Uh, sure. Of course I've played."

"Cool. Go ahead and pick out a racket, then."

Bryan looked down at the selection, totally lost. "All right. Well, this one here looks good."

"You sure you want that one? Let me see your grip?"

Bryan stared at him with a look of confusion.

"Take hold of the handle like this," Trevor said. "Now slide your index finger of your other hand in between the tips of your fingers and your palm. There, like that. No, that's too small of a grip. You need a racquet with a thicker handle."

"I do?" Tennis was beginning to seem more complicated than Bryan had imagined.

"Now, there are several other factors to consider when choosing a racquet."

"How about you just pick one out for me?"

"You sure? I thought you said it was a sissy sport. You sure you trust my judgment?"

Bryan slugged him playfully, laughing. "Okay. I take it back. Are you gonna teach me or what?"

Trevor drove Bryan to the country club. It was the golf course where his dads had memberships. "Just a word of warning," Trevor cautioned, "there's a lot of snobs who come here. Technically, they don't discriminate, but once in a while there'll be someone who gives attitude 'cause our dads are gay."

"Then why do you come here?" Bryan asked. Why support a place that condoned discrimination of any kind?

"Well, like I said, officially they're inclusive. It's like anywhere else. Even at school you're gonna run into a homophobe every now and then. They have a zero-tolerance policy, but you can't always fix stupid."

"I hear that."

"One thing about this place, though, is that money trumps all other factors. Regardless of race or orientation or whatever, if you're perceived as rich, everything's cool."

Bryan made a face. "I'm not sure I like that any better than the homophobia."

Trevor turned to look at him. "Man, there's something you should know about me. I'm not some rich kid. I grew up in a trailer park, and I hate that kind of snobbery. Adam's not like that either, and neither are Dad and Father."

"Why do you call them that? Just to tell them apart?"

"I think of 'em as my dads, and when Adam was growing up, he called Jeff 'Father' and Brett 'Dad.' That's how he always referred to them, and I guess I just got used to hearing it. But if you wanna call them by their first names, I'm sure they wouldn't care."

"Ya know, my dad's pretty cool, and if not for my mom, I bet he wouldn't even care I'm gay."

"Maybe he'll come around, then."

"I doubt it. My mom would kill him if he went against anything she said. She thinks I'm on my way straight to hell. She even got the church to send me a letter when I was staying at Evan's house. It said they were removing me from their membership because of my immoral lifestyle."

Trevor reached over and squeezed Bryan's hand. "Dude, I'm sorry. But ya know, if you wanna go to church with us, you're welcome. Father goes every Sunday, and sometimes Adam and me go with him."

"Really?"

"Yeah. Not all churches hate gay people, ya know."

"I think Adam's pretty lucky."

Trevor smiled at him. "Nah. I'm the lucky one."

"I think you're both lucky to have each other."

"True dat, but hey, you just got here. I bet you'll meet someone."

Bryan shook his head. After what had happened between his ex-boyfriend Liam and him, he didn't want to get his hopes up. Besides, he had to focus on his education and his mental health. The last thing he needed was another heartbreak. He didn't think he was strong enough to go through that again.

Trevor led him into the club, where they signed in. He gave Bryan the grand tour, showing him the points of interest, including the bar, the main dining room, the gym, pool, sauna, driving range, golf pro shop, and finally the locker room.

"You can share my locker today," Trevor offered, "unless you want your own."

"I'll share."

Trevor opened the locker and tossed his duffel inside, then removed his lightweight jacket. Bryan did the same, and once their personal items were locked up, Trevor led the way out to the courts. Trevor actually proved to be an excellent teacher, and he very patiently explained everything to Bryan.

"Dude, you're pretty good, for it being your first time."

"You think so? But you kicked my ass."

"Duh. Of course I kicked your ass, but just 'cause I'm awesome doesn't mean you're not good."

"Gee, thanks." Bryan turned to glance over at Trevor as they headed back to the locker room. They both were dripping with sweat. Just as Bryan turned his head, a tall guy about his age walked through the door, carrying a bottle of water. Bryan collided with him, causing the guy's water bottle to slosh onto his polo shirt.

"Dude! Watch where the fuck you're goin'."

Bryan stepped back and looked at the guy, sizing him up. He flushed as a wave of anger surged through him. He could tell the guy was one of those snobs Trevor had warned him about, just by the way he was dressed and the way his hair was so perfectly coiffed.

"Chill out, dude. It was an accident."

"Maybe if you paid attention where you were walking, dude!"

Bryan had an urge to slug him. What an arrogant fuck.

"Greg," Trevor said, quickly stepping between them. "We're sorry 'bout that. It was my fault, really." Bryan looked over at Trevor. Apparently he knew the guy. "Greg, this is Bryan. He's with me, and it's his first time here."

Greg glared at him. "Hmm, well… look, sorry I freaked out. It's just been, ya know, one of those days."

"I hear ya," Trevor said. "Are you all right?"

The tall, slender tennis player sighed. He was carrying a racquet bag and a duffel and was dressed in tennis sneakers and shorts. And his legs—well, they looked fine. Bryan took in the sight of him. Obviously he had money, and there was no doubt he was a cocky, stuck-up bastard, but with looks like that, no wonder he was a bit on the arrogant side.

He held his hand out to Bryan. "Can we start over?"

Bryan took a deep breath, then extended his hand. "Sure," he said begrudgingly.

"Bryan's staying at Adam's house, and he's going to University of Tampa. He's a basketball player."

"Seriously? That's awesome. And you brought him here to teach him how to play a real sport?"

Bryan's opinion of the guy lowered yet another degree. He glared at the pompous ass as Trevor laughed. "Hey, Bry's kind of sensitive about that sort of thing. And I gotta tell ya, he did awesome for his first time on the court."

"Oh yeah?" Greg looked Bryan in the eye, then trailed his gaze down Bryan's body. Bryan felt like he was being sized up, and gulped nervously.

"We gotta go," he said. "It was nice meeting you."

"You too, man."

"Sorry 'bout your, uh, peach-colored polo shirt. Hope it didn't get stained."

Greg shook his head. "It was just water, and it isn't peach. It's honey."

Bryan raised his eyebrows. "Okay. Well, see ya round."

"Maybe next time on the court," Greg suggested. "A little friendly competition, maybe."

"Maybe… or maybe not."

Greg turned to Trevor. "Well, man, good to see ya again. You take care."

They made their way into the showers, cleaned up, got dressed, and then headed out to the car. As they were walking across the parking lot, Bryan turned to Trevor. "Who was that guy? What an asshole."

"Greg? Oh, actually he's a pretty nice guy, and he's a hell of an athlete. He's probably gonna go pro."

"Seems a bit snobby to me."

"You think? Seemed to me he kinda liked you. Didn't you notice the way he was checking you out?"

"Trust me, I don't wanna be checked out by guys like him."

Trevor laughed as he approached the car. He clicked a button to release the door locks. "Is that why you were reading every inch of his body like a menu?"

"Shut up, I was not." Trevor opened the door and slid into the car. Bryan got in the passenger side. "I don't know what you're talking about. Didn't you hear the way he was talking to me? He has an attitude or something, like I'm beneath him."

"Or maybe he just thinks you're hot."

Bryan felt his cheeks getting warm. "You said he's going pro?"

"I'm not sure. You should ask him the next time we're here."

"Is he… ya know…."

"Does he hit for our team? Yeah, totally. He's head of the LGBT advocacy group at UT."

"Well, he's not my type. I don't like tennis jocks."

"Ah, I see. That's probably a good thing, 'cause it seems like he didn't much care for basketball jocks either."

"Good! I wouldn't want a guy like that being interested in me anyway."

But for some reason, Bryan couldn't stop thinking about him for the rest of the ride home.

CHAPTER
— 1 —

"AND HOW is your mood?"

Bryan looked up, albeit briefly, into the gray-blue eyes that seemed to be reading him like a book. If there was one thing he'd learned over the past year, it was how to get unwelcome attention. Very simple, actually. Just steal your parents' 9 mm with the intention of offing yourself. That little stunt had netted him months of ongoing therapy, a lifetime supply of happy pills, and a litany of labels he'd probably never be able to shake.

Nutcase. Whacko. Mentally unstable. Depressed.

Oddly, the one person he'd hoped would understand—his mom—didn't even seem to care. To her, it had been further confirmation that Bryan's life had completely derailed. She'd chalked up his thwarted suicide attempt to yet another symptom of his immorality. He'd turned his back on the Christian family values she and his father had tried to instill in him, and had exchanged them for a sinful homosexual lifestyle.

Now here he was in a different state, trying to begin a whole new life, but as a condition of moving, he had to continue with this pointless counseling. Sitting in the office of a brand-new therapist, this his second visit, he had to somehow convince "Hank" that he no longer had an overwhelming urge to hurl himself in front of a moving bus or leap from the closest tall building.

Dr. Weston had insisted he and Bryan be on a first-name basis, and so Bryan addressed him as Hank. Yet it didn't feel quite right, the man being old enough to be his father. And to be honest, Bryan really didn't want to be the doctor's friend. He didn't want to bare his soul to this person he hardly knew. He just wanted to be left alone so he could put the past behind him and get on with his life.

"Bryan?" Hank leaned forward in his chair, resting his elbows on his knees, and stared directly into Bryan's eyes.

Bryan looked away, then shrugged. "Good."

"Good?"

"My mood. It's fine."

"Bryan, how are you feeling right now?"

He resisted the urge to roll his eyes and forced himself to stare at the doctor's face. One thing he'd figured out was that these counselors liked eye contact. If you didn't stare at them, they thought you were hiding something, that you were dishonest or untrustworthy. Truth was, it just made him nervous. When he looked directly at someone, it was difficult to construct any kind of coherent thought. He seemed to forget how to speak like a normal person, and the words got tangled around his tongue. He could express himself much better if he didn't feel like the other person was staring at him, hanging on his every syllable.

So he'd learned a little trick. He looked directly at their forehead, or sometimes their eyebrows. Focusing on that one thing seemed to help, and they always thought he was looking into their eyes like they were doing to him.

"I'm okay," Bryan answered.

"Rate your depression for me, Bryan. On a scale of one to ten, ten being severely depressed, how do you feel *today*, at this minute?"

Why did these counselors think it was normal to use a person's name in every sentence? Real people didn't talk like that. And they sure as hell didn't ask each other to rate their feelings.

"Four, I guess."

"So a little down, but not bad?"

"Yeah. Um, I'm not thinking of doing anything foolish… again."

"Good." The doctor's sober expression seemed to belie the pleasant lilt in his voice. "And how about school? You getting settled in all right?"

"I've only had a week of classes, but it seems fine."

"Making new friends?"

"Uh… sure."

"You don't sound too convincing."

He took a deep breath and then refocused on the doctor's hairline. Maybe he wasn't *that* old. Thirty-five, perhaps. Hank was a friend of Adam's father. A gay-affirming therapist. One of the best, or so they'd told Bryan.

"I haven't met a lot of people yet. Like I said, this is only my second week."

"Have you considered possibly joining the LGBT student union? They have an advocacy group on campus."

"Maybe."

That was the group Trevor had mentioned, the one headed by that tennis star, Greg. Bryan didn't think it'd really be something that would interest him, especially not since Greg was the president.

"I think it might help if you became active in something. What about basketball? I know you played in high school."

Bryan had already decided he wouldn't even try out for the team. His hopes of an athletic scholarship had vanished when he messed things up back in high school, and his heart just wasn't in it. Fortunately, most of his tuition was covered by the scholarship Jeff had gotten him. He wanted to get a job and at least make an effort to pay something for his room and board. Jeff and Brett were letting him live in their home, which saved him a fortune.

"I'm looking for a job, actually. Not sure how much time I'll have for sports between studying and work."

"Well, Bryan, that's very noble. Staying focused on your education is important, but maintaining a social life is also important, especially to your mental health. I don't want you to recede into yourself. I think that could add to your depression."

They didn't get it. No one did. Being depressed wasn't something directly linked to how many friends he had. He'd had all kinds of people in his life back in Michigan, and yet he'd been suicidal. It wasn't about how many people were around him. It was about *feeling* alone. Did that even make sense?

"Trevor and Adam are my friends, and we do a lot of stuff together." Bryan felt like he had to defend himself all of a sudden, prove he wasn't a complete social retard.

The doctor nodded. "They're Jeff and Brett's sons?"

"Adam is. Trevor's his boyfriend, but he lives there too."

"Bryan, I want you to do something for me. Something that might be outside your comfort zone." Why was this man talking to him like they were best friends? "Over the course of this coming week, before our next scheduled session, I want you to make an effort to connect with someone outside your home. Strike up a conversation. Go to a movie. Talk to a classmate, maybe go out for a Coke or a bite to eat."

Bryan's pulse quickened a bit at the mere thought. "Um… you act like I'm antisocial or something. You know, in high school I was popular. I had a *lot* of friends." So why then was this so difficult?

Hank nodded, leaning forward a little more. "Absolutely, Bryan. I don't doubt that for a second, which is why I don't think I'm asking too much of you. It's not like you're an introvert. Think of it like riding a bike or driving a car. After you've suffered a fall or had an accident, it can be scary to get back on that bike or behind that wheel and go again. And I think that's what's happened with you. You've started to recede into yourself."

Bryan shook his head, willing himself to fend off the tears that were beginning to well in his eyes. He took a deep breath and straightened his posture. "You just don't get it," he mumbled.

"Then tell me, Bryan. Please."

How could he tell this man something he didn't even understand himself? How could he begin to put it into words? He'd gone from being one of the most popular kids in school to being an outcast. His own parents had rejected him, thrown him out on the streets. It was more than just falling off a bike. He'd had a complete wipeout.

"I'm not the same person I used to be. Things are different now."

"I don't agree with you, Bryan." Hank reached out and placed his hand on top of Bryan's. "Sure, you've changed. We all do, and it's a part of life. But at your core, you're not all that different. You've just matured somewhat. We've just got to find a way to convince you that the person you've always been is perfectly fine… just the way you are."

"HOW'D IT go?" Jeff smiled as he glanced over to Bryan, who'd just plopped himself into the passenger seat of the Prius.

Bryan shrugged. "Okay, I guess. He gave me this prescription." He held it up for Jeff to see.

"Oh, let's swing by the pharmacy and pick it up on the way home."

"Uh, you don't have to. I mean, if it's out of the way…."

"It's no problem." Jeff smiled. "I need to pick up a couple things while we're there anyway."

When they got to the drugstore, Jeff accompanied Bryan to the pharmacy counter, where they handed the clerk the prescription along with Bryan's insurance card. The middle-aged woman adjusted her glasses as she read over the scrip. Bryan wondered how she could even make sense of it. The handwriting looked like chicken scratch. The corners of her mouth curled as she looked up to make eye contact with Bryan. "Very well, I'll run this through, and it'll be about fifteen, twenty minutes."

What did people like that think of him? She probably wondered exactly how crazy he was to need antidepressant medication. That smile of hers was one of sympathy… or pity. He bit his lower lip and responded with a nod, then turned to Jeff.

"Come on. Let's browse." Jeff clasped a hand around Bryan's shoulder and offered an affectionate squeeze. Apparently he'd picked up on the nonverbal exchange.

As they were casually perusing the aisles, Bryan hung close to Jeff, but they didn't immediately speak.

"There's nothing to be ashamed of," Jeff finally said. "I was on meds like that myself at one time."

"You were?"

Jeff turned to him, looking right into his face, and this time Bryan didn't feel the need to break the eye contact. "I was about your age when I lost my mom. Well, actually, a couple years younger."

"She died?"

Jeff nodded. "And a bunch of other tragic things occurred. I thought my world was coming to an end. Fortunately, that was around the time I met Brett."

"Yeah, I remember from the play." My best friend, Evan, had starred in a play about Jeff and Brett called *Dumb Jock*. Evan's boyfriend, Noah, wrote the play after learning that Jeff and Brett had been students at our high school and Brett had come out to the entire school at a sports banquet the end of his junior year.

"Well, after Mom passed, I lived with my gram, but my relationship with my dad wasn't good. Even though I had Brett, I still struggled with a lot of grief issues, so my gram got me into counseling. And it helped. It really did, and so did the meds."

"But I haven't had a tragedy like that. Sometimes I... uh... I feel depressed and I don't even know why."

"And I think that's what the medicine is for. It'll help."

"Maybe I'm just crazy."

Jeff placed his hands on Bryan's shoulders and looked at him seriously. "You are *not* crazy. Depression is a treatable medical condition. Brett takes medicine for his heartburn and blood pressure, and this is no different."

"It just feels weird. This is the third prescription I've had since...."

"Sometimes it takes a bit of trial and error before they find the right medication."

Just then they heard Bryan's name over the loudspeaker. "That was quick," Jeff said, and they headed together back to the pharmacy.

"I'm sorry, but the insurance card has been denied," the clerk said, handing the card back to Bryan.

"Really? Are you sure?"

She nodded, frowning. "I'm sorry."

"Wait," Jeff said. "Bryan, this is your parents' policy, isn't it?"

"Yeah."

"Bryan's only eighteen," he said, addressing the clerk. "I know for a fact kids can remain on their parents' policies until they're twenty-six. It's part of the healthcare law."

She offered a sympathetic smile, then removed her glasses. "Yes, sir. That's correct, providing the parent chooses to do so."

"Why wouldn't they? It's a group family policy, and it won't cost them a cent to keep their son covered."

"You'd have to contact them, I suppose," she said. "All I know is that his name is not on the policy, and the prescription coverage was denied."

Bryan sighed. How embarrassing. "It's okay."

"No, it's *not* okay. How much is it?"

"Let me check, sir." She stepped over to her computer and then returned to the counter a few seconds later. "The prescription is three sixty seven."

"Three dollars and sixty-seven cents?" Bryan reached for his wallet. "I've got that…."

"Three *hundred* sixty-seven dollars," she clarified.

Bryan froze.

Jeff pulled out his wallet and handed her a credit card.

"Mr. Irwin! Er, Jeff. No, I can't…."

"You need your medicine. I'll call your parents when we get home. We'll get it worked out."

"I don't know what to say." He couldn't believe the man's generosity, especially after he'd already done so much. "I'll pay you back. I promise."

"We'll talk about it later." He placed his hand on Bryan's shoulder. "Don't worry about it."

CHAPTER
— 2 —

"HEY, SLICK, you ready?" Trevor stood in the doorway of Bryan's bedroom, watching as Bryan checked his appearance in the mirror. Should he wear a tie? Or were the polo and khakis dressy enough for a job interview at the country club? "You look fine," Trevor said, as if in answer to his unspoken question.

"I hate interviews," he grumbled. In truth, he didn't hate them at all. He was just nervous. With every passing day, his guilt grew exponentially. It was bad enough he was living off the generosity of virtual strangers, but now they were also paying for his medicine. "I just really hope I get this job."

"I bet you will." The optimism in Trevor's voice was almost enough to cause Bryan to feel hopeful. Almost.

Trevor was cute in a nerdy sort of way. His spiked, jet-black hair was a perfectly styled coiffure. Add to that his big brown eyes and oversized glasses, and he was the fulfillment of every gayboy's jock-nerd fantasy. Adam was lucky to have a boyfriend like Trevor. Shit, they both were lucky.

Bryan held out little hope of finding that kind of relationship. Not only did he lack the confidence to go out and meet a boyfriend, he also felt he just no longer possessed the social skills. Hank had encouraged him to reach out and at least attempt to befriend some of his new classmates, but Bryan had yet to even try.

He wished somehow he could go back to a time when things were easier. Back in Boyne City, when he was a star basketball player, he had lots of friends. He'd been a leader of sorts, and nobody had messed with him. His confidence had been at its peak, and Bryan had felt almost as if he were invincible.

Or had he?

No, he had to admit. It had all been an act. Overcompensation. The only real friend he'd had in Boyne was Evan, and Bryan had done everything in his power to utterly destroy that relationship. Yet in the end, it was Evan who'd stood by him. Evan had forgiven him for his disloyalty, and if not for him, Bryan probably wouldn't have survived.

Things had gotten better. He'd been offered an opportunity, a new lease on life. The generosity and compassion of strangers had saved him, but he still felt empty. He felt like an orphan, abandoned by his folks. Forgotten by all the people who'd once been so important to him. How was he supposed to pull himself up by his bootstraps when he wasn't even wearing any?

"You okay?" Trevor moved closer.

Bryan nodded, still staring at his own reflection. He looked incredibly tall next to his friend, but that was because Trevor was so short. He was short like Mr. Irwin—or Jeff, as he insisted Bryan address him.

"I think I lost you there for a minute," Trevor said, smiling warmly. "Trust me, you look great, and I know you'll get the job."

"Adam's dads are so cool," Bryan said. It was more like he was talking to himself than to Trevor. If only his parents were half as supportive and understanding….

"They are," Trevor agreed. "And you know they'd never expect you to work, not if you're not ready."

"Oh, I'm ready. I *need* to do something, Trevor. Something to remind me I'm not… I don't know…."

"You feel like you're mooching off them or something?"

He shrugged, then squared his shoulders and stared into the eyes of the smooth, clean-shaven face in the mirror. He no longer had a very high opinion of that person. He no longer wanted to *be* that person. "Well, to be honest, I *am* mooching off them. I'm living here for free, eating their food, using their house. They're even paying for my transportation and now my medicine."

"Bry, they *want* to do that. They're nice people."

"Yeah, I get it. But if even my own parents don't want me in my life, why—?"

"Because your parents are wrong." Bryan spun around. Adam stood in the doorway of the bedroom. "No offense, man, but your folks are assholes."

"Adam!" The intonation of Trevor's voice carried reprimand. "They just don't understand."

"No, Adam's right," Bryan said. "They really are assholes."

"They might come around," Trevor said, brimming with optimism. "People can change, ya know. My mom used to have a bad drinking problem. When Adam first met me, my life was pretty much crap."

"Yeah, I know. But with my mom and dad, it's different. They don't have a drinking problem. In fact, they don't really have any problems, other than me. I'm their one and only problem."

Adam leaned against the doorframe and crossed his arms over his chest. "Dude, if they can't accept you for who you are, that's *their* problem."

"That's easy for you to say." Bryan turned back to the mirror and smoothed out his shirt. "We should get going. I don't wanna be late."

As he stepped around Adam to cross the threshold out into the hallway, Adam reached up to touch Bryan's lower back. "Man, I'm sorry. I didn't mean to...."

"It's okay," Bryan said, shrugging it off. "Just don't forget how lucky you are. You have, like, the best parents in the world."

"And you're part of the family now," Adam reminded him.

Yeah. Whatever.

THIS WASN'T Bryan's first interview. He'd held other jobs back in Michigan, but when he was summoned into the manager's office, he felt intimidated in a way he hadn't previously. No doubt the opulence of his surroundings contributed to his insecurity. The large oak desk, leather chairs, and highbrow accoutrements that adorned the room reminded Bryan of the principal's office at school. He was just a college kid applying for an entry-level job busing tables or caddying on the golf course, not a job with a six-figure salary.

The office, like everything at the country club, smacked of materialism and pretentiousness. It was all about presentation, maintaining appearances, and when Mr. Carrington glanced up, staring over the top of his glasses, Bryan felt immediately as if he was being scrutinized. The balding, middle-aged man wore a navy pin-striped suit, and the corners of his mouth rose ever so slightly, as if he were trying to smile but couldn't quite manage to pull it off.

"Mr. Helverson, please have a seat." He looked back down at the paperwork in front of him, assessing Bryan's résumé and cover letter. "I see you come to us with some food-service experience. Are you interested in a position in our dining room?"

"Yes, sir," Bryan said. He cleared his throat, self-conscious about the way his voice seemed to sound an octave or two higher than normal. Nerves.

The manager looked up again, this time making eye contact, and Bryan willed himself not to glance away. Bryan smiled nervously, waiting for Mr. Carrington to continue.

"Why Meadowbrook? Surely there are plenty of area employers in the food-service industry eager to hire college students such as yourself."

This was one of those questions designed to test him. He was supposed to respond with something positive about the establishment, say how much he'd love to be a part of their winning team. Bryan felt his tongue thicken as he tried to formulate a reply.

"Uh. Well, sir, I visited Meadowbrook last week, used the tennis court with my friend. His dads are members. And I liked it. I liked the facility and thought…."

"Dads? Your friend has two fathers?"

Open mouth, insert foot. "Um, yeah. Or I mean, yes, sir. Well, they aren't exactly *his* dads. They're his boyfriend's." *Shut the fuck up! You're making it worse.* Bryan couldn't believe how stupid he was, blurting that out.

Mr. Carrington appeared unfazed. "I see. Who, may I ask, is the friend who sponsored your visit?"

Bryan swallowed and then took a deep breath. He sat up even straighter in the chair. "We were here on Brett Willson's membership."

"Ah, yes." Finally, a genuine smile. Mr. Carrington's face lit up with enthusiasm. "Brett and I go way back. And you know him through his son's friend?"

"Actually, sir, I know his sons through him and Jeff. I'm staying with them at least for this semester. They've been very generous, and I wanted to get a job. I need to, really, so I can at least offer them something, at least try to pay my way...."

He waved his hand dismissively. "You needn't explain. Well, Brett's reference is all I really need. I think with your food-service experience, you'd be most suited for our dining room. We'll start you as a server's assistant for your training, then advance you to a lead position once you've learned the ropes. The starting wage is ten fifty plus tips, with a two-dollar raise when you're ready to go it alone."

Bryan stared incredulously, his jaw dropping open of its own volition. "Wow. Or, I mean, that sounds awesome, sir."

"We'll start you this weekend. On your way out, speak with my secretary, and she'll give you the details." Mr. Carrington stood up and extended his hand. "Welcome to Meadowbrook, Bryan."

"Thank you, sir. Thank you so much!" He pumped the man's hand, smiling broadly.

BRYAN WAS beaming, unable to wipe the ear-to-ear smile from his face as he pushed through the exit door of the lobby. He pulled out his phone and typed a quick text to Trevor, declaring he'd gotten the job and was ready to be picked up. He then headed over toward the shaded area alongside the building to wait on one of the benches. When Trevor responded, he looked down to check the screen of his phone, and as he did so, he ran headlong into another pedestrian.

Sputtering, he glanced up, embarrassed and ready to apologize. Then he saw who he'd just run into. Again.

Greg.

The guy he'd met that first day he'd come to the club with Trevor. Just like their first collision, Greg again carried a racquet bag and duffel, and sported a pair of dark movie-star shades. He had an air about him like a Hollywood celebrity as he stood there with a hand on one hip, his bags hanging from his opposite shoulder.

"We meet again," he said. "We've just got to stop running into one another like this." He wasn't smiling.

"Man, um… I'm sorry. Really." Bryan felt like a klutz, but he was too excited about his good news to let it bother him. He shook his head and stepped aside, trying to sober his expression in order to appear sincere.

"It's okay, man. I won't lecture you this time about watching where you're walking." The way he said it sounded a bit like a lecture, or a mild scolding, perhaps. "You here with Trevor?"

"He's picking me up." Bryan was surprised the jock even remembered him. Greg was wearing a form-fitting white polo and khaki shorts, and he smelled like a fragrance ad from *GQ Magazine*. His sun-kissed tan and perfectly coiffed hair made Bryan wonder if he wasn't a model from said publication.

"Ah, I see. I was gonna challenge you to a game." He nodded toward his racquet bag.

"Sorry, maybe next time."

"Well, I didn't mean right now. I'm on my way to work, but I thought maybe after my shift…."

"You work here?" That was a shocker. Why would a rich kid like Greg need to actually *work*? His wealthy parents probably made him get a job to build character or something.

"Not here in this building, but next door at the restaurant. I'm just dropping off my bags. I store them in my locker so I can play after my shift. I'm a waiter."

That one statement immediately sucked the joy from Bryan's cheerful mood. "You're kidding."

With a somewhat bewildered expression, Greg shook his head. He reached up and removed his sunglasses, making eye contact. "No,

I'm serious. I've worked here for two years. That's how I pay for my membership."

"Oh. I just thought…."

"That I was some rich kid? Nah, I'm not that lucky. Not like *some* people." Was that some sort of accusation?

"Hm. Well, I guess we *will* see each other around then. I just got hired. I start Saturday in the restaurant as a server's assistant."

Greg shifted his stance, adjusting the shoulder straps as he smiled. "Imagine that. You'll be my trainee."

"*Your* trainee?"

"Server's assistant is just a highbrow term for newbie. You'll be paired up to shadow another waiter, your trainer. And since I'm scheduled Saturday, it'll probably be me."

"Fuck." Did he just say that out loud?

Greg laughed. "It won't be so bad. Trust me, a hard day's work won't kill you, and I'm not really all that bossy. Usually."

Just then Trevor pulled the car up to the curb beside them. "My ride's here."

"So why don't you guys come back around six? I can probably get another player, and we'll challenge you to a doubles match."

"I… uh… I already have plans. Maybe next time."

"Suit yourself. I'll see you Saturday, then." He turned and began heading for the entrance.

"See you then," Bryan called after him. "If I decide to even show up," he mumbled under his breath.

CHAPTER
— 3 —

TEN BUCKS an hour plus tips; that was unheard of in the food-service industry. There was no way Bryan could even consider blowing off the job, even if it meant he had to put up with an arrogant jerk like Greg. With any luck, the know-it-all hotshot wouldn't be Bryan's trainer. And what was up with him challenging Bryan to a tennis match? Trevor had told Bryan Greg was good enough to go pro, so why would he go around inviting newcomers like Bryan to play against him? Obviously it was an attempt to further stroke his ego.

As if an ego that size needed any stroking. He was hot, no question about it. He had a clean-cut, all-American look to him. Tall, slender yet toned body. From a physical standpoint, the guy was exactly the type Bryan found attractive, which was probably why Bryan was rock hard as he lay on his bed recalling his earlier encounter with Greg. He was still psyched about the job offer, and it felt great to be in such a good mood. Getting the job had been exactly what he needed. He'd been feeling depressed again, and he hated that frame of mind. He now had a silver lining to cling to, a bright spot in his otherwise gray existence.

It made no sense, really. He had every reason to be happy. Brett and Jeff had been wonderful, and so had their kids. He loved hanging out with Adam and Trevor, and he even had a pretty good schedule at school. He liked all his classes. There was no reason to feel sad.

Sure, his folks had disowned him, and that felt like crap. But a lot of people had assholes for parents. Most of them just dealt with it, got on with their own lives. So why couldn't he? Why did he get so overwhelmed, think all these negative thoughts about himself and his life, every time he was alone?

He pushed back the questions racing through his head, closed his eyes, and visualized Greg. Bryan didn't want to go there mentally, but he couldn't help it. He couldn't stop himself from replaying that mental image. That white polo shirt fit Greg so snugly Bryan could see the definition of his pecs. He'd even detected the ripple of his six-pack abs, and when Greg was walking away, Bryan had caught sight of his perfectly shaped bubble butt. Yeah, he was a god. A jock god.

Why'd he have to be such a cocky bastard?

With his eyes still closed, Bryan reached down and slid his hand into his khakis. The last guy he'd been with was Liam, and that was back in Michigan. He and his right hand were developing a very intimate relationship. That was fine, though. When he was going through puberty, he'd felt so guilty for pleasuring himself. His church had taught him masturbation was a sin. Though not as bad as fornication or homosexuality, it had still been frowned upon, and Bryan always felt the need to pray for forgiveness after he'd done the deed. He'd put all that behind him when he finally came out as gay. Now he jacked off whenever he felt the need, and he refused to feel guilty. Most of the time he succeeded in suppressing the shame. Most of the time.

When he felt depressed, an orgasm was one thing that truly provided relief. The rush he experienced was temporary, only lasted a couple minutes, but sometimes that was all he needed. It kept him from wallowing too deeply in his cesspool of self-pity.

That was the worst thing about his condition—the knowledge that it was self-imposed. Nobody liked someone who went around feeling sorry for himself. Even Bryan got annoyed by people like that, but he *was* one. People liked optimists. The hero in every movie was the person who refused to be defeated, who chose to look on the bright side and face their adversity with a positive attitude. Why couldn't he be like that? Why'd he always feel so blue?

Greg was probably one of those cheerful people. After all, he was head of the LGBT student advocacy group. He was popular. A leader. He must be pretty smart too. He was the whole package—looks, brains, and personality. A walking wet dream.

Bryan thought about those broad shoulders, those narrow hips. He thought about the sweat trickling down the side of Greg's jaw as he swung the tennis racquet. Fuck!

He leaned over the side of the mattress and retrieved the hand towel he'd hidden under the bed. He wiped up his mess and tucked himself back into his jeans. "I can't believe I just did that," he whispered. He'd jacked off while fantasizing about someone he wasn't even sure he liked. Saturday was gonna suck.

ON FRIDAY, Adam drove Bryan over to the country club to pick up his work uniforms. He had to wear black dress slacks and a tuxedo shirt with a bow tie. They then headed for the mall, where Adam helped him find a pair of dressy yet comfortable shoes.

"Don't take this the wrong way, dude, but you have an amazing ass."

Bryan was standing in front of the mirror in his work uniform. He wasn't exactly sure how *to* take the compliment. He simply glanced over at Adam and smiled. "Well, Trevor might not be thrilled to hear you say that, but thanks."

"Oh, he says the same thing. I didn't say I wanted to tap it, I just said it's nice… 'cause it is."

"Oh my God. So, like, you've talked about my ass?"

Adam, who was lying on the bed tossing a baseball into the air and catching it, was acting far too casual. "We think you need a boyfriend."

"You're changing the subject."

"No, I'm not. We've talked about what a good-looking guy you are, and it's not right that you're single."

"Geesh. Gimme a break. I've only been here, what? Two weeks or less?"

"That's just it." He pushed himself up on the bed and sat on the edge of the mattress. "You've been *here* two weeks. You've barely left the house other than to go to class."

"That's about to change. I start my job tomorrow."

"Which is why we should do something fun tomorrow night when you get out of work."

"Um, I dunno." He was scheduled to work until nine, and he was already starting to feel the pressure of mounting homework. He had a shitload of required reading and two assignments due by Monday. "Maybe, if I can get my studying done tonight."

"Dude, how much studying can you have already?"

"You wouldn't believe it, man. I swear these instructors must think we have no life."

"Well, I already talked to Dad, and he gave the green light for us to have a pool party tomorrow. Trevor said you're gonna be working with Greg."

Bryan rolled his eyes. "Maybe. Hopefully not. If I'm lucky, I'll get assigned to train with someone else."

"Why? Greg's cool, at least from what I know of him. He seems like a nice enough guy, and Trevor said, ya know, there might be something between you two."

"Oh there's a lot between us. Like his snobby, know-it-all attitude. I can't stand that guy."

Adam laughed. "Thou dost protest too much."

"Huh?" Bryan shot him the evil eye.

"Hm. Well, if you get over your hatred of him, you should invite him tomorrow."

"Who said I hate him?"

"Um, *you*." Adam was grinning ear to ear. "You just said you can't stand him."

"Well, that's different. That's not the same thing as *hating* him." Bryan adjusted his tie as he again assessed his overall appearance. "These bow ties are fuckin' lame."

"Trevor's inviting our friends Galen and Todd, and I'm gonna invite some friends from school. It should be fun."

"I'll think about it, but don't count on me asking Greg. Besides, I highly doubt he'd have any interest in going anywhere I invited him."

Adam shrugged. "Guess you won't know till you ask." He got up and walked over to the door. "You should get your homework done tonight so you don't have to worry about it. I mean, if you want. That way you'll have the whole night free to socialize… and whatever…." He winked just before stepping out into the hall and pulling the door closed behind him.

Oh great. Now I not only have my first day on a new job to stress over, but I also have to worry about socializing with a bunch of people I've never met. But it'd give him an excuse to get to know Greg a little better. Did he even want to, though?

He turned around, then glanced behind him to check out the reflection of his ass in the mirror. *I really do have a cute ass.*

CHAPTER
— 4 —

THE FIRST part of Bryan's shift was nothing at all like he'd expected. He spent almost an hour filling out paperwork, then had to watch a series of coma-inducing training and orientation videos. All this took place in the confines of a small cubicle in one of the back offices of the resort. Three hours later he was given a break, and then he was instructed to report to the restaurant and ask for Martin, the dining room manager.

As he stepped into the kitchen, Bryan instantly experienced culture shock. The chaotic environment was nothing close to anything he'd encountered at his previous jobs. Everyone seemed to be incredibly busy, focused on their own tasks, yet shouting back and forth to each other. He had no idea who Martin was or even where to look for him.

Bryan stood there in the doorway for a moment, but that didn't last long, as a waiter practically bowled him over, carrying a large tray of food platters. "Sorry," Bryan muttered as he stepped aside.

At last he caught sight of the only person he recognized: Greg. Bryan didn't want to approach him, but everyone else seemed so busy. Greg was leaning over the counter, explaining an order to one of the cooks. "They don't want it medium-well. They want it medium, and they claim it's overcooked." He shoved the plate forward. "Please! Just redo it, will ya? It's not my damn fault they're picky."

Bryan stepped closer, a tad intimidated. At last Greg turned and noticed him standing there. "Hey," he said, still scowling. "Welcome to hell's kitchen."

"Um, I'm supposed to talk to Martin," Bryan explained.

Greg nodded, then glanced around. "Over there." He pointed to a stocky, middle-aged man who was standing in the kitchen talking to one of the cooks. "Hey, Martin," Greg called out. "New employee here."

The manager looked up and nodded, then held up a finger to indicate it'd be a minute.

"So, um, do you know if I'm gonna be working with you?" Bryan asked.

Greg squared his shoulders, straightening his posture. "Don't know. Probably. If not me, it'll be Ian, and you'd better hope it's not him."

"Really? Who's Ian?"

"He's the one who trained me, if you wanna call it that. He made me work the first two hours of my shift in the storeroom. Had me take every canned good off the shelf and shake it up, then restack it on the opposite wall. Said it was a necessary part of rotation."

Bryan couldn't help himself. He grinned. "Do you guys always initiate the new guy by hazing him?"

In spite of himself, Greg smiled. "Nah. Well, maybe a little. I usually make the newbies do more of the shit jobs, ya know."

Bryan offered an understanding nod. "Kind of goes with the territory. I expected something like that."

Greg leaned in, and in a much lower tone, spoke directly into Bryan's ear. "Ian's a bit of a closet case, I think. He's always saying homophobic bullshit, but I think it's because he has issues of his own."

Sounded familiar. Bryan remembered being that way himself back in high school. "Are you sure? Maybe he just hates gay people."

"That's possible, but if that's the case, it's even worse."

Just then, Martin finished his conversation and walked over to them. "Martin, this is Bryan," Greg said.

"Bryan Helverson," Bryan said, extending his hand.

"You two know each other already?" Martin asked.

"Uh, yes sir. A little. We met last week at the tennis courts."

"Ah, so we have another tennis player." Martin rolled his eyes, then smiled. "We have a bit of a rivalry here. Half the staff thinks tennis is the only valid sport, and the rest of us normal people favor golf."

Bryan bit his lower lip, biting back an urge to express his true feelings about both lame sports.

"Nah, Martin. Bryan here's not a fan of tennis. He's a basketball player."

"A *basketball* player? It's about fuckin' time we got a real athlete."

Bryan started laughing. "I pretty much like most sports, but I haven't played much golf. Couple times with my dad."

"As long as you know the basics," Greg explained. "That way when the customers strike up a conversation, you can at least pretend to be interested."

"Listen to Greg, here," Martin said. "He's the master when it comes to schmoozing customers."

"You want Bryan to work with me, Martin?"

"Long as you don't mind splitting your tips."

Greg's mouth dropped open, and Bryan couldn't tell if either of them was serious.

"Look, I didn't expect to make any tips right away...."

Both Greg and Martin cracked up. "Don't worry," Greg said, "he's just kidding. He's trying to get me riled up. You'll get a chance later on to serve your own tables and make some tips, but for now you'll just be shadowing me."

Martin placed his hand on Bryan's shoulder. "So I'll leave you in Greg's capable hands. Work with him for the remainder of your shift, and he'll ease you into everything."

"Well, I already learned everything I need to know from those helpful training videos." They both stared at him incredulously until Bryan smiled. "Just kidding."

Quickly enough, Bryan learned that Martin wasn't exaggerating about Greg's customer-service skills. He exuded the warmest, most genuinely charming personality Bryan had ever seen. Making eye contact with each customer, he was truly engaging though not syrupy sweet. He even seemed skilled at defusing annoyed or cranky customers, always keeping things professional.

"Did you see how that woman was flirting with you?" Bryan whispered as they pushed through the kitchen doors.

"She wasn't flirting with *me*. I was flirting with *her*."

"Dude, she's like old enough to be your grandma."

"Didn't say I wanted to bone her. People just want to feel special, like someone's genuinely interested in them."

Bryan couldn't help but wonder if Greg did this with everyone. He'd been friendly enough so far, but maybe it was just an act. "What about the guys? Are there a lot of 'em who, ya know…?"

"Probably more than the women." Greg stepped up to the computer and motioned for Bryan to type in the order. "Go ahead." Bryan, who'd quickly taken to the computer system, tapped onto the touch screen and entered the information. The hardest thing about it would be remembering everything without writing it down. "Once you have the menu memorized, it'll be easier," Greg assured him. "Wait, she doesn't want a loaded potato. She wants butter and sour cream on the side." Greg showed him the buttons to modify the standard order.

Bryan shook his head. "I don't get how you just remember all these details."

"I use something about the person, something unique, and then associate that mentally with what they're ordering."

"What do ya mean?"

"I don't know. I just do it. Like that lady, the one you said was flirting, I remember her big hair. And I can visualize it in my mind, and I remember she wanted her potato toppings on the side and wants her iced tea with no lemon."

"And all that you associate with her big hair?"

Greg shrugged. "It's like a mental categorization. You have to keep it organized in your mind since you're not writing it down. Form a mental picture, I guess."

"You ever screw up?"

"Not usually. Most of the time, when the order is messed up, it's because they didn't tell me what they really wanted. But even if that's the case, you have to take the blame and apologize."

"That sucks," Bryan said.

"Customer's always right, ya know."

"Not!"

Greg laughed. "Well, we both know that shit's not true, but you gotta make them think that. And yeah, there are a ton of flirty gay guys who come in here. Most of 'em have money, and they're really good tippers. All you have to do is just give them some attention and smile a lot. Make 'em feel like you love to please them, and they'll lay out some pretty awesome tips."

Bryan cringed a little. "That's kind of gross," he admitted.

"It's customer service, not prostitution."

"But you're saying I'm supposed to act like a hustler or something just to get a tip?"

"No, you're supposed to act like a good server. You don't have to be a whore. Just be friendly and charming, and that's really all most of them want. Believe me, the older gay guys are gonna appreciate how good-looking you are. That alone is enough…."

Bryan stopped typing on the computer and turned to him. He couldn't believe what Greg had just said. "You think…."

"Hot stuff coming through!" Greg stepped closer to Bryan to avoid getting clipped by a big tray behind him.

"That's Ian," Greg said, after the server had pushed through the door. "He can be obnoxious." Greg was still within inches of Bryan, his body pressed closer than it needed to be. Bryan tilted his head back to look up into Greg's blue eyes. He inhaled, noticing Greg was wearing that same intoxicating cologne.

"Uh… didn't the other lady order the white fish?"

BY THE end of his shift, Bryan realized Martin had not been exaggerating when he'd said Greg was a master of customer service. And Greg's air of cocky self-confidence appeared to be based on something substantive. Bryan had at first viewed him as a know-it-all, but at this point he literally did seem to know it all. And from what Trevor had told him, Greg was the same way on the tennis court.

Bryan wanted to hate him, to be jealous of Greg's brains and talent. He wanted to resent his charm and good looks, mainly because everything within Bryan told him that guys like that—the ones who were so perfect—were really jerks. But it didn't seem like Greg was a jerk at all. It appeared that in addition to his good looks, intelligence, and talent, he also had a terrific personality.

Bryan stood alone in the bathroom, splashing his face with water as he gazed at his reflection in the mirror. "This is fucked up," he chastised himself. "You're acting like a teenage girl. He's just a normal, ordinary guy, like you. He's just a damn waiter and college kid." *But, damn! He looks fine in those snug-fitting black dress pants and that tuxedo shirt. And that smile of his, it fuckin' practically melts my heart every time he flashes it at me.*

They'd only worked together for five hours, and the time had flown by far more quickly than Bryan could have imagined. Usually the minutes at work, at least in the jobs Bryan previously had held, ticked by so slowly. But it felt like his shift had just started. He really didn't want the day to end, didn't want to punch out and go home. That would mean he'd no longer be with….

The door pushed open, and Bryan turned his head to see Greg step through the threshold.

"Hey, you all right?"

"Yeah." He pulled a strip of paper toweling from the dispenser and dried his face and hands. He hoped like hell Greg hadn't overhead him talking to himself.

"You did a great job today," Greg said as he stood there, neither stepping toward an open sink nor an available stall. Bryan felt self-conscious for a second, certainly unworthy of the praise being offered him. He'd made a few mistakes—nothing major, just newbie errors. He had a ways to go before he was even half the server Greg was.

"You're a pretty good teacher," he mumbled.

"What?" Greg's tone was incredulous. "Can you say that again a little louder?"

Bryan rolled his eyes, then smiled. "You can be a nice enough guy when you're not acting so... so full of yourself."

Greg's broad grin morphed into outright laughter. "That's the nicest backward compliment I've gotten today."

Bryan shrugged, then just stood there, waiting for Greg to step aside so he could exit and give his coworker some privacy. But when Greg finally moved, it was to position himself even closer to Bryan. Bryan gulped nervously, staring directly into Greg's blue eyes. "Sorry, I mean...."

"You mean sometimes I come across a bit too cocky?" Greg had lowered the timbre of his voice and was practically whispering.

A chill traveled down Bryan's spine as he nervously wiped his sweaty palms against the smooth fabric of his dress pants. "N-no. I didn't mean it like that. I just... uh. I just sort of had a different impression of how you'd be, and now that we've, ya know, worked together and stuff."

"You now realize what an awesome guy I really am." Greg leaned forward and reached up to place the palm of his hand against the wall above Bryan's head, more or less trapping him in Greg's personal space.

Bryan nodded. His eyes grew wide as he stared into Greg's perfect face.

"Well, it's an act," Greg confessed. "I'm not all that. In fact, half the time, I think it's just overcompensation."

Whatever it is, you do it well. Aloud, Bryan simply said, "Yeah."

"I know you're my coworker and my trainee, and, well, it's not exactly appropriate for me to do this, but...." He leaned in even closer and pressed his lips against Bryan's.

Bryan gasped, then quickly slid to the side, pulling away from Greg's kiss. "Hey, you wanna go to a party tonight?"

Bewildered, Greg spun around and leaned against the wall. Bryan stepped back, but continued to look at Greg's face.

"Huh?"

"Adam and Trevor are having a party at our house. A pool party, and they said I could invite someone."

Greg nodded, but didn't say anything.

"I just thought maybe you'd wanna stop by…."

"I'm an idiot," Greg said, shaking his head.

"N-no. No, it's okay." He obviously felt as if Bryan had rejected him. God, that wasn't the case at all. Bryan wanted it; he wanted nothing more than to kiss the drop-dead gorgeous jock. But it was so soon. "Look, I wouldn't invite you to my house if…."

"If you really thought I was an obnoxious, know-it-all coworker who'd cornered you in the bathroom on your first day and tried to put the moves on you?"

Bryan smiled as he felt the heat flare in his cheeks.

"It's just… I haven't been able to stop thinking about you since we ran into each other the other day," Greg explained. "And this morning, I kept thinking, God, I hope Bryan gets assigned to work with me."

"Really?"

"I was pretty sure you were gay, mainly 'cause you're friends with Trevor."

"Was that the only reason?"

"And 'cause you always seem to be undressing me with your sexy eyes."

Bryan turned away, now genuinely embarrassed.

"Wait! God, did I just say that out loud?"

"Just shut up and come to the party," Bryan said as he stepped briskly to the door and pushed his way through. *Fuck! He kissed me and said I have sexy eyes!*

CHAPTER
— 5 —

THE LOGICAL thing would've been to just catch a ride with Greg, but Bryan didn't want to face him again. He'd invited him to the party but didn't want to pressure him into going if he wasn't really interested. Besides, Trevor had already planned to pick him up and was probably waiting in the parking lot.

As he pushed his way through the exit doors, he immediately spotted Trevor's car parked by the curb. Bryan rushed down the steps and climbed into the passenger seat. "Thanks for picking me up," he said.

"How'd it go?" Trevor was cheerful, as usual, and Bryan couldn't help himself. He broke out into a broad grin.

"It was awesome," he said.

"So you didn't end up having to work with Greg?"

"Uh…."

"You *did* work with him, and it was awesome. I fuckin' knew it!"

Bryan started laughing. "Dude, he kissed me!" He grabbed hold of Trevor's wrist and squeezed it excitedly.

"What? No way!"

"Well… sort of. He started to, in the bathroom."

Trevor's mouth dropped open, then he laughed. "Oh my God. That's… uh… surprising. What'd you do?"

"I fuckin' freaked, man. I started to, like, kiss him back, then pulled away. It just sort of took me by surprise. And then I invited him to the party."

"Oh, cool. So he's coming?"

"I dunno. I ran out of there and punched out for the day before he could answer."

"Seriously? So this just happened?"

"Yeah. I'm an idiot, right?" He shouldn't have bolted like that. He should have stayed at least long enough to get an answer from Greg.

Trevor shook his head. "No, I think it's more like he's the idiot. I mean, it's kind of hot he kissed you like that, but on your first day? And in the john?"

Bryan laughed. "There was this weird tension between us. It just kept building up, and I think we both felt it. And he said he'd been thinking about me ever since we met the other day. And he just sort of lost control. And, and, and…."

"Breathe!" Trevor was grinning from ear to ear. "You're really cute when you get excited."

"Let's just get out of here before he walks through that door and sees me sitting here blabbing to you like this."

Trevor put the car in gear and pulled away from the curb as Bryan fastened his seat belt. "Do you think he'll show up?"

"Oh, if he cornered you in the bathroom and tried to kiss you, I'm positive he'll show up."

"Really? But I didn't even give him our address."

"He's friends with Adam. I'm sure he knows where we live."

"Fuck!"

"I thought you *wanted* him to come?" Trevor chuckled.

"I do, but still. Fuck!"

"YOU GUYS remind me of Adam's parents. No offense or anything, but… well, you know, the whole jock-nerd thing."

Galen took hold of Todd's hand and squeezed it, then with deadpan seriousness, replied to Bryan's statement. "Are you calling me a nerd?"

Todd glanced over at his boyfriend with a reproving look, then chimed in himself. "I take that as a compliment. I can't think of anyone I emulate more than Jeff Irwin."

Do people really use the word "emulate"? Bryan nodded seriously, or at least as seriously as possible, though he had this incredible urge to burst into laughter. He'd been on cloud nine since he got out of work. When he got home, he'd showered and changed, then he'd texted his best friend Evan to tell him about his first day at work.

One good thing about modern technology was the ease of keeping in touch. He texted or e-mailed either Evan or Noah several times a week. Evan had been Bryan's best friend since childhood, and Noah was his boyfriend. He was lucky to have friends like that, and now here he was in Florida with a whole new group of people surrounding him.

People probably assumed he was moody, given the way he felt so blessed and thankful for the amazing people in his life at one moment and then the next so overwhelmed with sadness and depression. He didn't understand it himself. He didn't know why some days he felt so alone, as if he didn't have a friend in the world. Self-pity? If that was all it was, it ought to be easy enough to snap out of. It was merely a matter of choice, deciding to look at the glass as half full.

At least tonight was one of those times he felt great, on top of the world. He was riding a high from the positive experience he'd had the first day of his new job. And he felt pretty awesome about the fact the hottest guy on the planet had tried to kiss him.

"Well, if you think about it, Adam and Trevor are kind of like that," Galen said. "Trevor's kind of an egghead, and Adam's a baseball jock."

It was true. In some ways, Adam and Trevor were like a modern version of Brett and Jeff. "Yeah, but they're such a perfect couple."

"Like us," Todd said cheerfully.

"Exactly," Bryan agreed.

"So you know what that means?" Galen asked. "It means we need to look for an available nerd for you to date."

Bryan started laughing. "You calling me a dumb jock?"

"Yes!" Todd and Galen said in unison.

Just then, Bryan looked across the room and saw Brett opening the front door. He smiled and stepped aside to usher in a guest who'd just arrived. Bryan's heart skipped a beat when he saw who it was.

Greg.

Greg and Brett stood there in the entrance chatting for a moment, and Brett placed his hand on Greg's shoulder. Obviously they knew each other. They were both smiling and laughing, probably talking about sports or the country club. Maybe Brett was commenting on his golf game, as he so often did. The din around Bryan seemed to fade as he took in the sight of Greg, freshly showered and changed, dressed appropriately for an evening pool party in his board shorts and silky Under Armor shirt.

"Hello! Earth to Bryan." Galen waved a hand in front of Bryan's face.

"Uh, sorry."

"You all right, man?"

"Yeah. Sorry, guess I just zoned out a second."

"Well, what do ya think? I can hook you up," Todd said. "Jeremy's in my statistics class. He's definitely a geek, but he's kinda cute. I think you'd really like him."

"Jeremy?"

"The guy I've been talking about…."

Bryan hadn't heard a word of it, nor did he even care, because at that moment Greg spotted Bryan and began making his way across the room. They established eye contact, and Greg started smiling.

"Uh, sure. I wouldn't mind meeting him. If you'll excuse me…."

As he took a few steps toward Greg, he heard Todd behind him, saying something to Galen about Bryan obviously not being all that interested in dating a nerd. But nothing anyone said really mattered just then, as Bryan nervously slid his hands into his pockets and bit his bottom lip. All of a sudden he felt conspicuous and strangely shy. The way Greg was looking at him made him feel as if he were on display.

Greg's smile was warm and inviting, and as he approached, he, too, seemed a bit uncharacteristically apprehensive.

"You made it," Bryan eked out.

"Yeah."

Bryan felt awkward, not knowing how to greet his new friend. A hug? Fist bump? Greg placed a hand on Bryan's shoulder and squeezed. "Of course I made it. I couldn't leave things like that."

"It's cool." What else was there to say? "Wanna go outside to the patio?"

"Sure," Greg said, "but I should say hi to Adam and Trevor." He glanced around, looking for the party hosts. He waved and nodded to a few of the other guests.

"I think they're out there already. Do you know Todd and Galen?" Bryan nodded toward his new friends, who were still standing a few feet away.

"Hey, man," Greg said, stepping over and clapping Galen on the shoulder. "What're you guys up to?"

"We were just getting acquainted with Bryan," Galen said. "Then you walked in, and he ditched us." Todd slugged Galen playfully on the bicep, apparently scolding him for his tacky attempt at humor.

Bryan's face warmed as Greg laughed. "Well, can you blame him?"

"I'm sorry," Bryan said. "I didn't mean to ditch you. I was just... um... I just noticed Greg when he walked in, and I wasn't sure he was even coming...."

"Todd was trying to set Bryan up with his friend Jeremy, a computer nerd from school."

Greg scowled.

"Well, we were talking about how all the jocks seem to have nerdy boyfriends—"

Greg held up his hand in a Vulcan salute. "Hey, I'm a fan of Star Trek. Does that count?"

"Look, I don't need anyone setting me up, but I appreciate the offer. I just got out of a relationship not long ago."

"Oh," Greg said, his tone conciliatory. "I didn't realize…."

"But you're single *now*," Galen said. "Young, hung, and full of—"

"Pizza!" Brett announced, carrying a stack of pies across the room toward the dining room table. They must have arrived right after Greg.

"Come on," Greg said, "I'm starving."

The four of them loaded up paper plates with pizza slices and then headed out to the patio, where most of the other guests had congregated. The dance beat booming from a nearby stereo helped to set the mood as some of the young guests mingled with each other while others splashed around in the huge swimming pool. The foursome congregated near a poolside table, where Adam and Trevor soon joined them.

"Wow," Greg said, "you guys really know how to throw a party."

"Dude, we're glad you made it," Adam replied. "How's the tennis game?"

"Got a tournament coming up in two weeks. Shit, it's killing me, but I think I'll be ready."

Bryan wanted to connect with Greg, spend time with him one-on-one, but as the party kicked in, he started to withdraw more into himself. Greg, on the other hand, seemed to become more animated, interacting with everyone. Soon they were separated, Greg off in a corner talking to other people, and Bryan sitting at the patio table.

When he felt a hand on his shoulder, he turned to see Trevor standing behind him.

"You okay?" Trevor asked.

"Sure," Bryan said, offering a weak yet cordial smile.

"Wanna go for a swim?" Trevor suggested.

Bryan shrugged. "I can't. I just ate."

"That's an old wives' tale, ya know."

Bryan looked up to see Greg standing on the edge of the pool, now shirtless and ready to jump in. The overhead lights reflected off his smooth golden-brown skin tone. He was literally breathtaking.

"You really should go for it," Trevor whispered.

"Uh, I don't know. This whole thing, I'm not sure it was such a good idea. He's just… um… we're just too different."

"Oh really?" Trevor pulled up a chair beside him and sat down. "Well, in that case, you're right. Of course, two people who are different could never make it as a couple. Look at Adam and me— we're practically carbon copies of each other."

"You're so cute when you're sarcastic." It was true. Trevor really was a cutie, with his big glasses and spiked hair.

"Dude, don't be a moron. He *kissed* you, and now here he is at a party you invited him to."

"But he's barely said two words to me since he got here."

"Take your shirt off," Trevor commanded.

"What?"

"You heard me. Take it off, and get your ass over there in that pool."

"Trevor…." He tried protesting, but the look on Trevor's face said he wasn't about to take no for an answer. "But…."

Trevor shook his head and pointed to the pool.

"All right. All right." Bryan stood up and reluctantly peeled off his shirt. He then kicked off his sandals, took a deep breath, and squared his shoulders. "Here goes nothin'."

Bryan marched over to the side of the pool, looked down, and spotted Greg. He turned and looked up at Bryan, smiling. "How's the water?"

"Awesome," Greg said. "Come on."

"In that case, look out below!" He then proceeded to leap into the air, tuck his knees against his chest, and drop, cannonball style, into the water right beside Greg.

As he came up for air, he heard Greg cursing. "You bastard! You're gonna pay!"

Greg exacted his revenge by diving underwater and pantsing Bryan. Fortunately, he was wearing briefs, but it was embarrassing nonetheless. Bryan pulled his pants up, dove toward Greg, and tackled him, pulling him underwater. When they came up for air, Bryan was breathless and staring into a set of brilliant blue eyes. The feel of

Greg's bare skin against his own gave rise to goose bumps along Bryan's arms. They stood there for a moment until Bryan at last pulled away. He then picked up a basketball he found floating in the water, spun around, and made a shot into the poolside net mounted on the opposite end of the pool.

"Damn!" Greg exclaimed. "Impressive."

Of course, that then prompted Greg to retrieve the ball and try a shot of his own. He missed, but it was close. Before long, they were engaged in a friendly game of one-on-one.

"You wait," Greg threatened. "We both know this isn't a fair matchup. But when I get you on the tennis court, I'm gonna kick your butt."

Soon others joined in, including Adam and Galen, and it turned into more of a formal game with teams. Bryan's team won by a landslide, so far ahead that they eventually stopped keeping score. Water basketball proved quite different from actual basketball. With no dribbling the ball and no fouls called when players tackled or splashed their opponents, Bryan had the perfect excuse to wrap his arms around Greg's athletic torso and pull him underwater. Bryan also fell victim to such attacks from Greg on several occasions, even a couple times when he wasn't in possession of the ball.

A couple hours later, they were the only two left in the pool, still splashing around and laughing hysterically. When they finally dragged themselves from the water, Greg was visibly trembling, apparently shivering from the chilly night air.

Bryan laughed. "Hey, I'm from Michigan. This sixty-five degrees is like a heat wave to me."

Trevor was standing by the patio table and handed Greg a big, blanket-sized towel. "Sorry, last one. You two will have to share."

Bryan shot Trevor an incredulous look, but Greg took it in stride, slid beside Bryan and draped the towel around his shoulder, then snuggled next to him. They sat down together on a patio bench.

"Where is everyone?" Bryan asked.

"Bunch of 'em are downstairs playing video games, and a few people left already."

Bryan looked around and realized the patio was empty. "Oh geez. I guess we got a little caught up in our game."

"It's cool. I was watching. You guys are pretty fierce competitors."

Greg was holding the ends of the towel together with one hand in front of them. He slid his other hand around Bryan's back and pulled him closer.

"I think I'll go find Adam," Trevor said, then winked. "It *is* getting a little chilly out here."

"I'll be in in a little bit."

Trevor rolled his eyes before turning away. He turned back, just before sliding open the glass door that led into the house. "Take your time and make sure you're dried off. Dad gets a little testy when we track water in from the pool."

Bryan laughed as Trevor pulled the door closed behind him, then grew quiet. No longer were the sounds of other guests and music surrounding them. At last it was just he and Greg.

"We got off to a rough start," Greg said, staring into Bryan's eyes.

"Yeah. About that—I'm sorry."

"Believe me, I know how I can come across. It's just, well, I've kinda learned that if I don't have faith in myself, no one else is going to. I think to some people that seems cocky."

Bryan nodded, then looked down toward the floor. It was difficult, even in this intimate moment, to sustain eye contact. He understood exactly what Greg was saying. He knew it better than anyone, but for different reasons. He truly wished he could be like that, confident and sure of himself.

"I shouldn't have come on to you today at work like I did, though."

Bryan grinned as he remembered. "You surprised me."

"I know. I surprised myself, but it wasn't cool. I was supposed to be training you."

"Maybe you were trying to train me on kissing."

"Maybe."

"I guess I didn't do so well with my first lesson."

"Oh, you did all right, but I hope we can schedule some future training sessions."

Greg released his grip on the towel and reached up to place his fingertips beneath Bryan's chin. He tilted Bryan's head back slightly, causing him to look up into Greg's eyes. "I really like you, and I wanna get to know you better."

Bryan was now trembling, but he knew it wasn't from the cold air. He was quite warm, snuggled beside Greg's nearly naked body. Greg caressed his back, gently making small circles. That touch coupled with the soothing sound of Greg's voice created a warmth in the center of Bryan's chest, a peaceful, calming sensation that helped to ease his anxiety.

"You're shaking," Greg said.

"Sorry." Bryan felt self-conscious, embarrassed.

Greg leaned in and kissed Bryan softly on the lips. "Hey, it's okay. I'm not going to hurt you."

Bryan smiled. "I know. I… uh… I'm not sure why I'm acting so skittish. Stupid, really. Like a girl or something."

"No. Vulnerable."

Greg was right. He did feel vulnerable, partly because of what he'd been through, and partly because of the rejection he'd experienced. And then the failed relationship with Liam hadn't helped. Then being sent to the psych ward had impacted him, left a scar that couldn't quite heal. If Greg knew the truth about him, who he was and what he'd done, he wouldn't be so interested. He wouldn't be interested at all.

"I've been through some stuff. That's kind of why I'm here."

"It's cool. We all have a past."

Bryan took a deep breath, then released it slowly. "You know how you said Ian was a closet case?"

"Yeah."

"Well, that's how I was for a long time. Years, in fact. Then my best friend came out. His name is Evan."

"He was your best friend back in Michigan?"

"Yeah. We grew up together, neighbors since kindergarten. God, when we were kids, we were inseparable. In the summer, we always slept at each other's house. If he wasn't staying over at mine, I was at his. We loved the same sports, had all the same interests. It was weird, kind of like we were brothers or something."

"That's pretty awesome. I wish I'd had a close friend like that." Greg's smile felt genuine.

"We were on the same team. Evan was the captain, and we won the state championship for our division in our junior year. It was awesome."

"Wow."

"But then everything changed. Evan shocked all of us when he came out. He kissed this other guy in front of a whole group of people. On stage."

"Really? Like at a concert or something?"

"No. It was a play. See, Jeff and Brett are originally from my hometown. And Evan's boyfriend Noah wrote this play about them. Evan got the lead role, playing Brett, and Noah was playing Jeff. They had to kiss in one of the scenes, but Evan kissed Noah for real and told everyone he was gay. It was a really big deal, created a shitstorm of epic proportions."

Greg laughed. "Fuck, that's pretty cool, though."

Bryan couldn't help grinning. "It was, even though I didn't think so at the time. I was devastated. I couldn't believe my best friend would do something like that."

"'Cause it embarrassed you?"

Bryan looked away. "Nah. Because…."

"Because it *hurt* you."

He felt a single tear trickle down his cheek and shook his head slightly. "It's stupid."

"Bryan, it's not stupid. You loved him. You were in love with Evan."

He nodded. "Crazy, isn't it? I really did love him. I loved him with all my heart, but he had no way of knowing. And the way I treated him—it was awful. I called him a faggot, tried to get him kicked off the team."

Greg wrapped his arm around Bryan's shoulder and pulled him in close, cradling him against his chest. "But he forgave you. He understood...."

"He shouldn't have forgiven me. I didn't deserve it." He was crying freely now.

"Bryan, listen to me." Strong arms held him as he placed his head against Greg's smooth, hard chest. "Forgiveness is never deserved. If you'd deserved it, it wouldn't have been forgiveness."

"I know, and that's why it really sucks." Bryan pushed himself back, sitting upright as he wiped his cheeks. "I told you I was acting like a girl."

"Girls aren't the only ones who cry, Bryan. And you're not the only one who's done something you're not proud of. My dad died when I was thirteen, and I wasn't even there when he passed away."

"Oh God, I'm sorry." Bryan felt like an idiot, blubbering about his problems when they were nothing compared to losing a parent.

"No, it's okay. I've worked through it, but it was hard. I had to play that day. It was a tournament, and Dad insisted I go. I won, actually, and I was so excited. I couldn't wait to get back to the hospital with my trophy to show him. But when I got there...."

"You were too late."

He nodded. "I was so angry, pissed at myself for being so selfish, I threw the trophy across the room and smashed it against a cement wall. I swore I'd never forgive myself."

"But... but you were only doing what he'd asked. He told you to play."

"It didn't matter. What kind of a person goes out and plays a sport when his dad is in the hospital dying of cancer?"

"The kind who loves his dad and wants to make him proud."

Greg smiled through his tears. "Yeah." He bobbed his head slowly. "I know that now, but at the time all I could feel was guilt."

"You had nothing to feel guilty about."

"And neither did you. You loved Evan, and you were trying to sort out all those really complex, confusing questions about yourself. You struck out at him, and it wasn't fair. It wasn't the most mature thing to do. Just like it wasn't too grown up of me to smash my trophy. But sometimes we lash out when we shouldn't. It's all part of being human."

It really wasn't the same thing. Greg's dad had just died, and it was understandable he'd be emotional. But Bryan nodded in appreciation of his friend's empathy. "My dad won't even talk to me anymore."

"I'm sorry."

"Him and my mom are really religious. Born-again Baptists. They think I'm going to hell."

"I can't imagine what that must be like for you. I really am sorry."

"Hey, it's their loss. Right?" He'd gotten pretty good at pulling off the false bravado, but Greg seemed to see through it.

"I almost think it's worse than what I've lost. My dad's in heaven, but at least I know he loved and accepted me. My mom too; she's, like, my biggest supporter. I can't imagine what it'd be like to face rejection from my family. My mom and sister both support me and totally accept that I'm gay."

Bryan wasn't sure how to respond. He should say something like, "They might come around," or "At least there's still hope." But he knew that wasn't likely. When he was in the hospital, after he'd tried to kill himself, they hadn't even shown up. To them, he was already dead. They'd disowned him. Forever.

"I have a new family now," Bryan said. "Well, sort of...."

"Not just sort of."

Bryan and Greg looked up to see Adam and Trevor standing in front of them. He hadn't even heard them come out onto the patio.

"We *are* your family, and we always will be, man." Trevor moved closer and placed a hand on Bryan's shoulder.

"We're sorry," Adam said. "We didn't mean to invade your privacy, but when we peeked out the window and saw Bryan crying…."

God, how embarrassing.

"It's cool," Greg said. "And it's true, Bryan. You couldn't ask for a better, more loving and loyal family than you have here."

"Thanks, guys." He looked up into Trevor's eyes, then Adam's.

"Group hug!" Trevor said, leaning in to wrap his arms around Bryan. Then Adam joined them.

It wasn't the romantic scene Bryan had fantasized about, but it was perhaps the most beautiful experience of his life.

CHAPTER

— **6** —

"WHAT I'M hearing sounds promising, Bryan. You're making progress; wouldn't you agree?"

Hank sat with one leg crossed over the top of his opposite knee, reading glasses resting on his nose. He definitely looked the part of a priggish psychiatrist. Still, Bryan liked him, and there was something about his manner that was reassuring.

"I think so," Bryan agreed.

"Well, you've started a new job, made some new friends. How's school going?"

Bryan shrugged. What was there to say? School was school. Boring.

"It's all right."

Hank nodded, rocking back and forth ever so slightly in his chair. "I want you to be cautious with this new friend. Greg is his name?"

"Yeah."

"Sometimes when we're still working on personal issues of our own, it's more prudent to take new relationships slowly."

Bryan wanted to roll his eyes. Instead he just looked away.

"Bryan?"

He took a deep breath and then turned to again face the doctor. "Last week you said I should go out and make friends. I did, and now you're telling me not to."

"Oh, I encourage you to make friends. By all means, continue to interact with people and establish solid relationships. When I say to be cautious, I'm talking about romance."

"Well, I'm not even sure there is a romance. He just gave me a little, um, a little kiss. That was it."

Hank smiled, then removed his glasses. "I'm just saying, try not to rush into anything headlong. Take your time, get to know each other, and allow the relationship to develop at a reasonable, tempered pace."

Bryan didn't even know what that meant. How could he? Other than Liam, he'd never really had a serious boyfriend. And at this point, who knew what would happen with Greg?

"I didn't say we were in love or anything. I just like him, and for some reason, he likes me."

Hank immediately raised his hand, palm facing outward. "Whoa. What did you just say?"

"Uh, I said I like him."

"After that…."

"And that he likes me."

"*For some reason.* Bryan, why would you qualify your statement with that? Are you suggesting it's unreasonable for Greg to like you the same way you like him?"

God, he hated the way shrinks picked apart every little sentence. "No, that's not what I meant…."

"I think maybe it is. Maybe not consciously, but if you ever want Greg—or anyone, for that matter—to like you for who you are, you have to believe you're worthy. I'm sure you've heard people say, 'you can't expect someone else to love you if you don't even love yourself.' It's a trite saying, I know, but sometimes those kinds of sayings are grounded in truth."

"I *do* like myself," Bryan lied.

"Five things, right now. Quickly. Give me five awesome things about yourself that you absolutely love."

This time he did roll his eyes. "Seriously?"

"Totally seriously. Yes… go!"

He released a frustrated sigh then closed his eyes for a second. Five things. "Okay, I like that I'm a decent basketball player."

Hank nodded as he used his index finger to tick off one digit on his other hand. "That's one. Athletic ability."

"And I'm not a genius or anything, but I'm somewhat intelligent."

"Brains. That's two."

"I'm in decent shape. I have an all-right body, but I'd like to be a bit more toned. I've been meaning to get a membership at the gym. I might just start using the equipment at the country club."

Hank nodded. "Okay, good looks is number three."

"I didn't say I was good-looking. I said I have an all-right body."

Hank raised his eyebrows. "You're a good-looking young man. Move on. You have two more."

"Look, do we have to do this? Can't you just accept I like myself? I told you I do."

"Nope."

Bryan wanted to get up and walk out. He pulled out his phone to check the time. He still had twenty minutes left.

"We have plenty of time, Bryan."

What else was there to say? He could say he was a good friend, but that wasn't true. Look what he'd done to Evan. And now here he was taking advantage of these new people in his life, living off their generosity—their charity.

"My friends back home always said I had a good sense of humor."

"Okay, that's four. You don't sound too convincing, though."

"I dunno. I'm just different now, at least a little. I used to be more outgoing, the life of the party. I was the one who told all the jokes and was the center of attention."

"Well, I'm not sure at your core that your sense of humor has changed any. Like we talked about before, you've started to recede into yourself a bit. The whole point of making new friends was to address this. Over time, as you get used to your new environment, you'll come out of your shell again."

"Yeah. Maybe."

"One more. Try to make it a big one, something you're really proud of."

Bryan's frustration was quickly evolving into something far more intense. He no longer was just annoyed at the doctor for grilling him with these questions. He was genuinely getting angry.

"Look, I don't know. I can't think of things like that, off the top of my head. Why don't *you* tell me!"

The doctor nodded. "Fair enough. You're gay."

"What's *that* got to do with anything?"

"I asked you to name five things about yourself you liked. Don't you like the fact that you're gay?"

"That's like asking me if I like the fact I'm male or that I'm white. I'm gay. Big deal!"

Hank leaned forward in his seat. "You know that, and I know that. I'm positive you're aware of the fact your sexual orientation is simply a part of who you are, that it's not something you've chosen any more than your race or your gender. But just because you know it up here…." He pointed to his head. "Doesn't mean you believe it in here." He then pointed his finger toward Bryan's chest and maintained the gesture for a few seconds.

"You're wrong! I do believe it in here. I know I didn't choose to be gay, and I told that to my parents. I told them straight out, 'I'm gay. I was born this way!'"

"That must've been a huge disappointment for them."

"Bullshit! What right do they have to be disappointed? What fucking right do they have to make me feel like I'm *inferior* or something!" He was shouting and now visibly shaking. Hot tears streamed down his cheeks. "Goddammit!" He covered his face and released a sob.

Hank had moved over to the sofa and now sat beside him. He handed Bryan a box of tissues and rested a hand gently on Bryan's shoulder. "They have *no* right to make you feel that way. They have no right to feel that way themselves, Bryan. They're wrong. They're *absolutely* 100 percent wrong."

HE DIDN'T want to walk out of the office with his eyes all red. Jeff would know he'd been crying. Again. He stopped off at the bathroom and splashed his face with cold water. These counseling sessions were such bullshit. What good did it do to sit around and cry, feel sorry for himself? He considered asking Jeff if he could just cancel the counseling altogether. Since his parents had dropped him from their insurance, someone else was obviously having to foot the bill. Undoubtedly it was Jeff and Brett. Either that, or he'd be getting charged. Lord knew he couldn't afford something like that.

Jeff was cordial on the ride home, chatting amiably as usual.

"Mr. Irwin," Bryan said, a couple blocks from the house. "I mean, Jeff. Now that my insurance has been cancelled, who's paying Hank?"

"Oh, don't worry about it. We'll take care of it, at least until you get new insurance."

"Look, I don't want you to do that. Besides, I'm not sure I really need the counseling."

They were approaching the house, and Jeff reached up to press the garage door remote located on his visor. "Bryan, I can't force you to do anything you don't want to do, but I can ask you, as a favor to me, to continue at least a little while longer."

He hated that Jeff had phrased it that way. How could he deny the man a favor after all he'd done for him? "Sir, I'm not sure how that's doing you a favor. To me, it feels more like I'm just using you, taking advantage of your generosity."

"I wish you wouldn't feel that way, Bryan." Jeff reached over and squeezed Bryan's thigh, just above the knee. "You're not taking advantage. I want to make sure you're okay, that's all. And if you remember, the counseling was one of the original conditions."

Jeff was right. Bryan had agreed to see a therapist before he'd ever moved to Florida. He nodded. "Yeah, I know. All right, I'll keep going. But I'd feel a lot better about it if you didn't have to pay for everything."

"I'm waiting to hear back from one of your parents. We could get you signed up for insurance right now, but I'm not sure if they're claiming you as a dependent on their taxes. You just turned eighteen this year. After the first of the year, we'll get you enrolled based on your income. In the meantime, Brett and I can cover your bills. It's not a big deal."

"It really is. It's a huge deal. I want to start paying my way. When I get my first check, I'm giving it all to you."

Jeff smiled and shook his head. "No, you just hold on to it. Put it in the bank."

"Sir, please…."

"Okay, fine. You give me your check, and I'll hold on to it."

"Deal. I should make enough tips to pay for anything I might want or need, but I'll give the checks to you."

"That sounds fair." They were now in the garage, and Jeff opened his door. "Come on, I'll make us some lunch."

CHAPTER

— **7** —

BRYAN'S NEW job was going well, and he loved it. He really liked working with Greg. For his first three days, they worked alongside each other. Bryan maintained his own tables and functioned fairly independently, but he knew Greg was there to answer questions and offer direction. After work, on the third day, Bryan went with Greg to the tennis courts. Greg hadn't exaggerated his ability. He was good, damn good.

Afterward, they showered separately, and Greg offered Bryan a ride home. When he stopped the car in front of the house, they sat there for a few moments talking.

"I don't know much about tennis, but I bet you'll kick ass in that tournament," Bryan said.

Greg reached over and took hold of Bryan's hand. "I hope so. I just wish you could be there to watch."

"I will, if I don't have to work."

"Yeah, but with you being new, you probably will be scheduled. The opening match is on a Saturday."

"Well, maybe I can make it to some of the other matches."

"Bryan," Greg whispered, "I don't wanna talk about tennis."

Bryan laughed nervously. His heart was racing, and he felt like a schoolgirl on her first date. "Okay. What *do* you wanna talk about?"

"I don't want to talk."

As Greg leaned toward him, Bryan closed his eyes and felt the soft pressure of Greg's lips against his own. He responded, opening his mouth slightly, and pressed back. He reached up with his left hand and cupped the back of Greg's head as the kiss grew more passionate.

"Oh God," Bryan whispered when he pulled back.

"I don't want to rush you."

"Please...."

And they kissed again, this time even more fervently. Greg tasted of mint gum and smelled like that heavenly cologne he always wore. Bryan was swept away by the kiss, to the point of practically swooning. He also was aroused, and wanted more from Greg than he'd ever do in a parked car. He felt Greg put his hand against his thigh, inching closer to the bulge that was now throbbing inside Bryan's dress pants.

"You taste so good," Bryan said. He didn't know what else to say.

"You too," Greg whispered, carding a hand through Bryan's hair. "And you feel good too."

"I... uh... should probably get inside."

"Yeah," Greg said, but he made no effort to pull away. "Probably, before this goes too far."

"What if... what if I want it to go further?"

"Not yet." Greg leaned back and smiled at him. "Let's just take it slow, get to know each other. I haven't even taken you on an official date yet."

"Are you asking me out?"

"I'm off Friday, but you're scheduled till nine."

"It'll be my first day working without you."

"You'll do fine. You're more than ready. Ian can help you with anything you don't know."

Bryan hadn't yet really interacted much with Ian. "Ian... the closet case."

"He'll be all right. He won't give you any shit at work."

"I hope not."

"I'll pick you up Friday after work, and we'll have our first date. We can celebrate your first night flying solo at work."

"I'd like that." Bryan smiled, then squeezed Greg's hand. "I'd like that a lot."

"Okay, it's a date, then."

"Okay," Bryan said. He reached over for the door handle, then quickly changed his mind and leaned in for one more kiss. "Bye!" he said quickly as he pulled away and pushed open the door.

WHEN FRIDAY finally came, Bryan was nervous for more reasons than one. He was working alone, without Greg's guidance, and then they were going on their first date. He didn't know which to stress over more. But work went well, and with the help of a coworker—Traci, a waitress who also happened to attend UT—he made it through the entire shift without incident. At the end of his shift, he encountered a problem. He glanced around, looking for Traci, and spotted her in the back of the dining room, serving a table. Just then, Ian walked by.

"Ian, can you show me how to redeem one of these gift cards?" Bryan asked. It was the first time he'd seen anything like it.

"Gift cards? You mean gift *certificates*?"

"Uh, yeah." They were by the register, and Bryan was trying to close out the customer's ticket prior to the end of his shift. "This is the first one I've gotten."

Ian laughed, but it wasn't in a friendly, carefree sort of way. It came across as derisive. "I fucking hate working with new people," he said. "Especially when they weren't properly trained. Just leave it and I'll do it, but I get half the tip."

"What?" Bryan stepped back and looked him in the eye. Ian was a little shorter and more slender than Bryan, and everything about him set off Bryan's gaydar, including his softer mannerisms and nasally voice. "Forget it. I'll ask Martin."

"Martin's not gonna like being bothered, especially over something so lame. You're just gonna get your *boyfriend* in trouble for not training you right."

This time Bryan laughed. "It's okay, I'll take my chances. I think Martin knows what a good trainer Greg is, or he wouldn't have scheduled me with him. And by the way, he's not my boyfriend." Bryan turned to head further into the kitchen to look for his boss.

"He fucked me, ya know."

Bryan stopped dead in his tracks. Slowly he turned around. "What are you talking about?"

"Greg. He fucked me, just like he wants to do to you, if he hasn't already. It's obvious… kind of pathetic, though."

"You're gay, then? I thought you hated gay people."

Ian's laugh was more like a cackle, like the Wicked Witch of the West. "Is that what he told you? Let me guess: he said I'm a closet case."

"Yeah." His reply was only a whisper.

"Figures. Guess that's one way of keeping you away from me. If he'd said he was my ex, you'd realize what a slut he is. You know, I'm not the first, either. Every new guy who works here, Greg puts the moves on. The first day I worked with him, he tried to get me to blow him in the men's room." Ian had lowered his voice, as if telling a dirty little secret.

"You're lying," Bryan said, but he didn't believe the words he was saying. It was far too specific an accusation to be a coincidence. Greg had tried to make advances on Bryan in the bathroom, and on his first day. And he'd said Ian was a homophobic closet case.

Ian stood there, arms crossed over his chest. "Never mind. Come here and I'll show you how to do the fucking coupon."

"I… uh… you do it. You can keep the tip. It's time for me to punch out." He spun around and dashed back into the kitchen, then pushed his way through the rear doors into the employee breakroom where the employee lockers and time clock were located.

His head was throbbing, and his vision blurred as his eyes filled with tears. What a fucker! What a lying, miserable bastard. He wondered if everything Greg had told him was a lie. And here Bryan had trusted him, poured out his heart to him, told him all he'd gone through.

He slumped down in one of the chairs and leaned forward, crossed his arms on the table in front of him, and buried his face in the crook of his elbow. He couldn't believe Greg would be so deceptive. If all he'd wanted was a fuck, why didn't he just come right out and say that? Was Bryan anything more to him than just another conquest? And why had Greg lied about Ian? Why hadn't he told Bryan the truth about having slept with him?

He lifted his head when he felt a gentle touch against his back. "Bryan, are you all right?" Traci was leaning over him, her voice quiet, filled with concern.

"Uh, yeah. Just tired." He wiped his eyes and cheeks with his fingertips.

"Here." She pulled out a napkin from her apron, then slid into a chair beside him. She rested her hand on his shoulder, then gently slid it down his arm, caressing it. "Did that ass hat say something to you?"

He shook his head but did not answer.

"Well, I want you to tell me if he did. Ian can be a little shit. I saw you two talking, and then you rushed back here."

"I'm sorry," Bryan finally said. "How embarrassing." He couldn't believe he was sitting here crying in front of one of his coworkers.

"Bryan, what'd he say?"

"It doesn't matter."

"It *does*."

He took a deep breath then turned to look at her. She had such a pretty face—cherubic, almost. And penetrating blue eyes. She looked like a china doll. "You're really pretty," he said.

She smiled broadly. "You're avoiding my question, but thank you."

"No, I mean it. Well, um, I should tell you…."

"You're gay."

"How'd you know? Am I that obvious?"

She shrugged and cocked her head slightly to the right. "Nah, I guess I just have gaydar or something. And I kind of caught you checking out Greg's ass the other night."

Greg. Bryan winced at the reminder.

"Hold it. Did Ian tell you something about Greg? Listen, whatever he said, it's bullshit. Greg's a nice guy. I've worked with him for over a year, and I can tell he really likes you."

"Did he used to go out with Ian?"

Her smile slowly faded, then she squared her shoulders and sat upright in her chair. "I'm not sure what their history is, Bryan. I think they might have gone out for a short time. Probably just long enough for Greg to figure out what a douche bag Ian is."

So it was true. Greg had gone out with Ian, and he'd lied about it.

"But try not to hold it against Greg," she added. "Haven't we all dated a loser or two in our past?"

"I don't really care about his past, Traci. I don't care who he's dated, but…."

"You need to just forget whatever Ian said to you. It's probably not true, or not *completely* true. Talk to Greg."

"I dunno. I guess I'm not really ready for any kind of serious relationship right now."

"That's understandable." She nodded. "I'm kind of in the same place right now myself. On the rebound. I just want my space. Some me time."

"Exactly," he agreed.

"Sweetie, I think you've gotta go back and finish closing out your register. Ian was spouting off about it, bitching that you took off without settling your shift."

"Shit."

"It's no big deal. If you need help, I can walk you through it."

"That'd be awesome. Hey, do you think you could give me a ride home?"

"Sure." She leaned in and wrapped her arm around his shoulder. "Come on, let's get the hell out of here."

CHAPTER

— **8** —

BRYAN CANCELLED his date with Greg via text message, then turned off his phone. He didn't want to face Greg, and he certainly didn't want to hear any more of his lies. He knew he'd have to face him eventually, being that they were coworkers, but he'd deal with that later, when the time came.

Hank would be happy. He'd warned Bryan not to jump into a relationship right away. And Bryan was relieved on some level. It was better to learn the truth about Greg now than to find out later. He should have gone with his gut. He'd sensed that first day he'd run into Greg at the country club that he was a player. Then Bryan had let Greg schmooze him with smooth talk. Greg had flirted with Bryan and told him all that mushy, sentimental stuff about his dad being sick and dying. He wondered now if any of it was even true.

"You know what sounds good right now?" Traci was behind the wheel of her Honda Civic, driving Bryan home.

"Huh?"

"Chocolate ice cream."

"Yeah, that does sound good. Or a hot fudge sundae."

"Hell, yeah. Now you're speaking my language. Let's go to Bruster's, my treat."

"Bruster's? That's an ice cream shop, I take it."

"The best."

"Cool, but you should let me treat you since you're giving me a ride… and since you've been such a good friend."

"You sure got changed fast." Bryan had brought a change of clothes to work with him, planning to change after his shift. He'd wanted to look good for his first date with Greg.

"I'm supposed to be on a date right now." He looked out the window, grimacing, as his chest tightened. In spite of his anger, it still hurt.

"I'm sorry," Traci said, reaching across the seat and rubbing her fingers against Bryan's forearm. "You know, it's not too late. You could call him, get his side of the story."

He shook his head, refusing to look at her. He knew if he turned to face her, he'd get emotional again. "It doesn't really matter. I'm not ready to jump into a serious relationship right now." His statement was resolute enough to nearly convince himself.

"Who said anything about a serious relationship? I thought it was just a date."

"Uh, yeah. It was supposed to be, like, our first official date. Last weekend we went to a party together, though. Or, actually, it was at my house, and Greg showed up."

"And you had fun?"

"We had a blast, and…."

"And he asked you out."

Bryan sighed. "Oh, I love this song. Can we turn it up?"

"Really? I love Pink, too. But you're changing the subject." She reached up and pressed the stereo's power button to turn off the radio. "I know I'm butting in, and I shouldn't. But you don't know Ian the way I do. Seriously, you can't trust him. Whatever he said to you…."

"It's not just what Ian said." Ian had merely confirmed what Bryan had originally suspected. Greg was a big man on campus, head of the LGBT student union, semipro tennis star. He was out of Bryan's league. And why would Bryan have expected anything different from him? He was hot-looking and popular, and he'd probably dated a lot of guys. What was wrong with that? Bryan just didn't like the way Greg had been dishonest with him. Why hadn't he said he'd gone out with

Ian rather than making up that shit about him being a closet case? "When I'm ready to date again, I want it to be with someone who's more like me. Greg's too... I don't know... too everything. And I'm just, like, this average joe."

Traci laughed. "Is that how you see yourself?"

They'd arrived at the ice cream shop, and she maneuvered the car into an empty parking space. It was a white brick building with a large red-and-white canopy hooding the walk-up order windows. The establishment reminded Bryan of the Dairy Queen restaurant back in his hometown, with its billboard menu and outdoor seating. The round metal picnic tables each had their own umbrella.

"What do you mean?"

"Average. You think you're just average?"

He shrugged, then pushed his door open. "Well, I am, compared to Greg."

"Not!" she said as she stepped out of the car. They each walked around the side of the vehicle and met on the curb. "Bryan, Greg obviously doesn't agree with your self-assessment, otherwise he wouldn't have asked you out."

"From what Ian said, he asks a lot of guys out."

She grabbed hold of his arm. "That's bullshit. There's no rule against a single guy going out with more than one person, is there? And it's not like he's a slut, at least not from what I've seen. I think at one time he was interested in Ian, and they went out together. But when Greg found out what Ian was really like, he broke things off. Now Ian's gone all psycho, insane with jealousy, and is trying to start some shit. If he can't have Greg for himself, he doesn't want anyone else to have him."

Maybe it was true, but it really didn't matter. Bryan couldn't get the image of Greg and Ian out of his head. He thought about what Ian said they'd done in the bathroom.

They walked over to the window, and Bryan quickly perused the posted menu. "I'm gonna get one of those waffle cone sundaes," he said. "With hot fudge."

"The hot fudge brownie sundae is so good." She stepped up to the window and placed the order. Before Bryan could protest, she paid the cashier.

"I thought I was paying."

"I told you this was my treat." She smiled as she turned to him, giving Bryan her full attention. "Do me a favor. Call him. If you don't, you're gonna regret it. Besides, you still have to work with one another. Even if you don't go out with each other, you're gonna want to maintain his friendship."

"I've got to work with Ian too, and I have no plans to *ever* be his friend."

"Shut up and just call him." She placed a hand on her hip as she stared him directly in the eye.

After they got their sundaes and took their seats at one of the picnic tables, Bryan reluctantly pulled out his phone. It wouldn't hurt to turn it on and at least check his messages.

"Greg left me a voice mail," he said. A part of him said he should delete it, but Traci's expectant stare pushed him in the opposite direction. He pressed the button to connect to his message box, then put the phone on speaker.

"Hey, Bryan… um, I got your text, and I'm sorry you're not feeling great. When I showed up to pick you up from work, Martin told me you got a ride home from Traci. It's no big deal. We can reschedule our date, but I wanna make sure everything's okay. I'm gonna head over to your house… see you in a few."

"Shit." Bryan sighed. "He's probably there now." Now everyone was going to find out what had happened, including Trevor and Adam.

"I told you Greg's a decent guy. God, this ice cream's the bomb." Bryan hadn't even touched his own sundae, and the ice cream was starting to melt. "Just call Greg and tell him you two need to talk."

"I don't know."

"Do it!" Just then, Traci's ringtone chimed. She picked up her phone and read the screen. "It's him, texting me."

"This is crazy. He's stalking me…."

"He's not stalking you." She laughed. "He found out you'd left work with me, and when I didn't take you straight home, he probably got worried."

"What'd he say?"

"He asked if you're with me."

"Don't reply!"

Her thumbs flew across the touch screen, rapidly typing a response as if she hadn't heard him. "I'm telling him to come have ice cream with us."

"Traci!"

"You'll thank me later."

Bryan sat there stewing and moving his plastic spoon around inside the waffle bowl. Traci was right; the ice cream was really good, but Bryan didn't feel like eating. He dreaded the confrontation with Greg and feared it would escalate into something ugly. Then again, he really wasn't all that angry anymore. He felt embarrassed, and his ego was bruised. He didn't want to play the victim, but he couldn't help but feel hurt.

Maybe he was making this too much about himself. As he thought about it, there wasn't really any logical reason for him to be upset that Greg had dated someone else. They hadn't even known each other when Greg had gone out with Ian. And Greg was under no obligation to disclose his romantic history to Bryan, at least not yet.

When Greg whipped into the lot and parked his car beside Traci's, Bryan looked up and made eye contact with Greg. He raised his hand and waved meekly as Greg swung open his car door and got out. Damn, if he didn't look even sexier than Bryan imagined he would. He was wearing a T-shirt that fit him so snugly it looked like it had been painted on. Bryan closed his eyes and exhaled, then took another deep breath before Greg approached their table.

"Hey, how you feelin'?" Greg said. He placed a hand on Bryan's shoulder and squeezed gently, then slid onto one of the bench seats beside him. "You're not feeling well?"

"Something someone said made him a bit nauseous," Traci said.

Bryan felt the heat flare into his cheeks. "Uh, I was just upset, and... um, I didn't think I'd be good company."

"Who said something, and what'd they say?"

Bryan shot a look directly at Traci, just as she was opening her mouth to speak. "It was Ian," Bryan said quietly. "He told me about…."

"About us? Him and me?"

Bryan nodded. "And I'm just a little bit confused. Why didn't you mention that you'd gone out with him instead of saying he was a closet case?"

"Maybe I should get going and give you two your privacy," Tracy said.

"Wait. Please stay," Bryan said. His duffel bag was in the backseat of her car, and he wasn't sure how this conversation with Greg was going to work out. He didn't want to have to call Trevor for a ride if he got stranded. Plus, he needed her for moral support.

"It's okay, Traci," Greg said. "You already know about the situation with Ian, and you can back me up."

"I already told Bryan that Ian's a drama queen. He's just trying to get back at you."

"And he has no reason," Greg said. Bryan could see the anger and frustration in his eyes. He pursed his lips and tightened his jaw, and Bryan sensed he was about to explode. "Bryan, I don't know what he said to you, but I can almost guarantee you it was bullshit. I did go out with him, and maybe I should have told you. But I never lied to you. I said Ian's a closet case, and he is."

Bryan shrugged. "Doesn't seem too closeted to me. In fact, he seems the opposite, like he goes around flaunting his sexuality."

"In front of certain people, yes. But the biggest issue I had with him was that he's a total hypocrite. When he's with some people, he tries to act 'straight.'" Greg raised his hands to gesture air quotes. "Says all kinds of homophobic shit and acts like being gay is something to be ashamed of."

Bryan could relate to that. It was exactly how he used to be, and not that long ago. "Maybe he hasn't fully accepted his own identity."

"Or maybe he's just a jackass. I don't know, and I don't really care. If that had been the only issue, we probably could have worked through it. But he's also a liar, and he does mean things, things to deliberately hurt people."

There was something more to the story, something Greg wasn't telling him. "He said you came on to him on his first day of work, that you tried to get him to… um… blow you in the bathroom." He'd lowered his voice and quickly glanced over to Traci, afraid he shouldn't have said it in front of her. She placed her elbows on the table and rested her chin in the palm of her hands, looking directly at Greg in anticipation of his reply.

"Bull! I told you, he's a liar! I never came on to him. In fact, he's the one who put the moves on me, and when he cornered me in the bathroom, I told him no. We ended up going out later that week, but we never did *any*thing at work. I swear!"

"But on my first day…."

"I kissed you, and like I already said, I'm sorry. I should have waited."

"You kissed him on his first day?" Traci said, smiling. "That's so sweet."

"Ian made it sound like it was something you do with a lot of the new employees. Like I was just another conquest or something. I'm sorry, but I thought…."

Greg took hold of his hand. "It's not true." He shook his head. "Ian and I only went on one date, then I broke things off with him. We never were even officially a couple, and I haven't gone out with anyone else from work. Ever."

"Really?"

"Ask Traci."

"I already told him," she said. "But, Bryan, I can see why you thought what you did, why you believed Ian. Greg kissed you on your first day of work, and then when Ian made it sound like that's what he does to all the new guys…."

"But I don't! I swear, Bryan."

"He said you lied, told me he was a closet case so I would steer clear of him and not find out about him being your ex."

"That doesn't even make sense. I knew you'd find out eventually, and when the time was right, I was gonna tell you. But we haven't even had our first date yet. I wasn't about to start talking about my exes."

"I'm sorry." Bryan felt like a fool. "I should have just waited until I talked to you."

"It's not your fault," Greg said. He slid off his bench and onto the seat Bryan was using, then wrapped his arm around Bryan's shoulder. "I know how Ian is, and if I'd been in your situation, I'd probably have believed him too."

Bryan leaned against him, placing his head against Greg's shoulder. He reached up and rested his hand against Greg's solid pecs. "So you're not mad?"

"Oh, I'm mad, but not at you. Wait till I see Ian again."

"I think I really should give you two your privacy." Traci stood up. "You should go ahead and go on your date."

"My bag's in your car," Bryan said.

"Come on," Greg said. "You look amazing, by the way."

"So do you."

Greg leaned over and kissed him softly on the lips.

"Aww!" Traci said, clapping. "You two are such a cute couple."

Bryan pulled back and turned to her, smiling ear to ear.

CHAPTER
— 9 —

"I DIDN'T wanna take you to a fancy restaurant. Fuck, we work in one."

"I like this so much better," Bryan replied, and then he stuffed a handful of fries into his mouth.

"Burger Monger has *the* most awesome burgers."

Bryan didn't disagree, although he had to admit he never thought he'd be holding in his hands a burger that weighed a full pound. Halfway through, he realized he probably wasn't gonna be able to put away the whole thing.

Greg laughed. "You look like you're about to explode."

"Thank God I didn't eat much of that ice cream."

"Least you got a taste of your dessert first. That's the thing about eating here. You're too stuffed to even think of food again for at least a couple days."

Bryan smiled at the gorgeous jock sitting across from him. In this light, Greg's eyes seemed to sparkle a radiant blue. Like the ocean. "I can't believe I almost fucked this up." He spoke more to himself than to Greg, but Greg responded by taking Bryan's hand in his own.

"I wanna take you somewhere after we leave here."

"Okay."

"Here in Tampa, there's this place called Pride Center. It's like an LGBTQ headquarters. They have all kinds of stuff going on there, and there are a bunch of gay businesses in the area. We call it Pride Park."

"I think I heard Jeff or Brett mention it."

"Yeah, well, I pretty much know everyone there at the center, mainly because I'm involved with the student union at UT." Greg was being modest. He was the student union president. "And they have *the* most awesome youth group you could ever imagine."

Bryan squinted, then cocked his head slightly to the side. "What's that got to do with us? Aren't we too old for a youth group?"

"They have a group for thirteen- to seventeen-year-olds and a separate group for people our age, eighteen to twenty-one. The idea is that even though we're technically adults, we're too young to do a lot of the stuff other grown-ups can do. We can't get into most clubs, which means no dancing or partying. Really limits the possibilities for a gay social life."

"That makes sense," Bryan agreed. "I guess I never thought of it."

"They meet once a week, and a lot of times they plan things for the weekends, like dances and shit. Usually they do one bigger event per month. Like, I think this month they are going to Busch Gardens."

"Cool. I haven't been there yet. My family used to vacation in Orlando sometimes, so I've been to Disney World. But until I moved in with Jeff and Brett, I'd never even been to Tampa."

"Well, it's not just the youth group that's cool. They have so many resources, and that place is always busy. They have exercise classes, bingo, dance classes, crafts, you name it. And they even have a department dedicated to mental health resources."

Bryan froze, then slowly released Greg's hand. He felt the smile fade from his face as his mood immediately sank. "Wh-why are you telling me that?"

"Oh, I didn't mean anything by it. It's just… well, you told me what you'd been through, and that you were struggling with depression."

"Yeah, well, that doesn't mean I'm mental."

Greg shook his head. "Of course not. But I know the guy who runs that department at the center. He's a really cool guy named Steve. And they have a support group that meets for people with depression and bipolar disorder."

"I don't *need* a support group." Suddenly Bryan felt defensive. It was embarrassing Greg would even bring up the topic. "I don't have bipolar disorder. I just, um, have been sorting through some personal issues."

"Yeah, I get it." Greg bobbed his head. "You know, I was seeing a counselor myself, after my dad died. I had a lot of anger and grief. It sucked."

Bryan finally exhaled, releasing some of his defensiveness. Of course, he should have remembered that. If anyone would understand Bryan's situation, it would be Greg. He'd lost his dad, so he definitely understood depression.

"How'd you get over it?"

"Mostly by talking about my feelings, and to be honest, I'm not completely over it. I wonder if I ever will be. When you lose someone you love, someone close, like a parent or sibling, I think it leaves a void that isn't easily filled. I'm not sure I even want it to be filled."

Bryan was surprised by Greg's openness. It took guts to admit he was weak. Then again, was grief a sign of weakness? Was depression? "I know what you mean. Well, not exactly, but sort of. My parents are still alive, but in a way it's like they're dead to me. Or maybe it's more like I'm dead to them. Some days I want to just completely forget about it, forget I ever knew them. Then other times I'm glad I have memories of a better time."

"Right." Greg placed his hand on top of Bryan's. "That's what I mean. It felt almost like a betrayal of my dad's memory when I forced myself to move on with my life. A part of me didn't want to let go of the sadness I was feeling. I thought that by doing so, I was forgetting him, disrespecting him, in a way."

"He would want you to move on, to be successful."

"Yeah, I totally get that. I knew it all along, at least in my mind. But in my heart, all I felt was the guilt."

"I guess it isn't exactly the same thing for me, because they're both still alive. I already know my life is a disappointment to them. *I'm* a disappointment."

"They might be disappointed in the fact you're gay. And because of their religion or whatever, they can't accept you. But I bet there are things about you that make them proud."

Bryan thought about it. Maybe Greg was right. Bryan's dad had always been proud of his athletic ability. His mom used to brag about him constantly. She even had one of those horribly embarrassing bumper stickers on her van that said, "My child is an honor roll student at BCHS." So why couldn't they see he was the same person? None of those characteristics they were so proud of had changed. He was still the same Bryan, but all they could focus on was his sexual orientation.

Greg took hold of Bryan's hand as they walked out to the car. "I hope I didn't upset you. I honestly don't think you're crazy, and there is nothing to be ashamed of for being depressed."

"I know," Bryan said, and then he squeezed Greg's hand. "I have a pretty full plate right now, though. With work and school, plus my weekly counseling sessions, I'm not sure I want to get involved with a support group."

Greg shrugged. "That's cool. I totally understand. I just wanted to make you aware it existed. I do think we should participate in the youth group, though. We don't have to go every week, but we can choose the events that interest us."

"I'm down with that."

Greg stopped walking, and Bryan followed his lead. They were a few feet away from the car, standing on the sidewalk. "Bryan, I really like you," Greg said. "I like you a lot, and I want us to be more than friends."

Bryan's heart pounded rapidly as he looked into Greg's eyes. "I like you too."

Greg leaned in and pressed his lips against Bryan's, delivering a searing kiss right there in front of Burger Monger. Bryan's spirit soared, and he reached up and wrapped both arms around Greg's torso, melting into his embrace.

He really did like Greg a lot, and he was beginning to wonder if perhaps it might be more than mere infatuation he was experiencing.

TREVOR WAS cracking up, practically to the point of falling out of his chair. "I can't believe you went to bingo on your first date! Were there, like, a million old people there?"

Bryan smiled, then nodded. "Yeah, come to think of it. But it was fun, and I won!"

"That is so cool," Adam said. "What do you win at bingo?"

"Money! I won two hundred thirty bucks!"

"That's insane," Adam said. "We should start going."

"Statistically, the odds are against winning or even breaking even," Trevor pointed out. He was a math major, after all. "I think it was a case of beginner's luck."

"I don't care what kind of luck it was," Bryan said. "I'm just stoked I won. Where's your dad at?"

"Downstairs," Adam said. "Probably watching another one of those sappy Hallmark movies."

"I wonder if he'd mind if I went down there. I need to talk to him."

"He won't mind," Trevor said, "but you're not getting away that easily, not until you give us every little detail of what happened on your date. Why'd Greg show up here looking for you, saying you'd cancelled on him?"

Bryan plopped down in an empty recliner, then raised his hands to his forehead and ran his fingers through his hair. "Oh God, that's a long story. This dude at work started some shit, said he was one of Greg's ex-boyfriends. He told me a bunch of stuff that wasn't true, and I kind of freaked."

"Ah, kind of how Trevor did the first time I kissed him."

"I did *not* freak!" Adam stared at him, raising his eyebrows. "Well, maybe a little. But you were pretty cocky, and I thought you hated me. When you kissed me, it took me by surprise."

"Exactly," Bryan said. "When Greg kissed me in the bathroom, it was the same way. I was like, where'd that come from? Then this Ian guy, Greg's ex, told me Greg did that same thing to all the new guys. He pretty much accused Greg of being a slut and made me think I was just some sort of conquest for Greg."

"Weird. I've known Greg a while, and I never knew he had a boyfriend named Ian." Adam was sitting across from him, leaning forward in his chair with his elbows propped against the armrests.

"They only went out on one date. I guess when Greg broke things off with him, Ian felt rejected and has been a shit stain ever since. He's trying to get even or something."

"I hate people like that," Adam said.

Trevor rolled his eyes. "How can you hate someone you don't even know?"

"All right. I hate that kind of behavior."

Trevor smiled smugly. "Well, I'm glad you talked it over with Greg and got it straightened out. I can tell he's crazy about you."

"You should have seen him when I got my bingo. He was more excited than I was, jumping up and down, pumping his fist into the air."

Adam and Trevor laughed. "I bet all those old people about had heart attacks."

"It wasn't *all* old people. There were a few younger people there. And they have a youth group at the center for people age eighteen to twenty-one. We're gonna start going."

"Really? I wonder how come Dad didn't tell us about that," Adam said.

"Probably because we have so much shit going on already," Trevor surmised. "School, sports, work…."

"That's what I told Greg. How am I gonna find any time for more activities? He's like the Energizer Bunny or something. He's involved in everything, and it's like everything he touches turns to gold. He's good at literally everything."

"*Every*thing?" Adam raised his eyebrows.

Bryan laughed. "I don't know quite yet, but I wanna find out."

With that, he pushed himself up and briskly stepped across the room toward the basement stairwell.

"WELL, YOU'RE all smiles. I'll take that as a good sign. Guess the first date went okay." Jeff was curled up on one of the leather sofas in the entertainment room, a book in his lap.

"It was pretty awesome, actually." Bryan took a seat in a chair opposite him. "We went out to dinner, then hung out at the Pride Center."

"Oh yeah. There's always something going on there. It's an amazing resource for the community."

"We ended up going to bingo. Can you believe that?"

"You know, I used to have a friend who liked bingo, and I go with her on occasion. Never really won anything, but it was fun."

Bryan shifted himself in the chair, so that he could get to his pocket. He shoved his hand in and retrieved a stack of twenty-dollar bills, folded in half. "Well, I won tonight, and I want to give you my earnings. Two hundred thirty dollars plus another seventy I made in tips." He leaned forward, extending his arm and holding out the money.

"Oh my." Jeff began shaking his head. "Why don't you hang on to that?"

"Sir, you promised you'd let me pay."

"I did?" He cocked his head and looked up toward the ceiling, thinking. "Hm, I guess maybe I might have said that."

"Well, you said you'd take my paychecks, and I'd just use my tips for spending money. But I haven't gotten paid yet."

"Oh yeah. Well, there you go. You don't have to pay me anything, then. Not until you get your first paycheck."

Bryan sighed and thrust his arm closer to Jeff. "Please take it...."

"But if you give me all the money you made, you'll have none left."

"I still have thirty bucks left over, and I work again tomorrow, so I'll make more tips. I feel like crap living here for free, and this is the first chance I've had to pay you *any*thing."

Jeff reached up, making a great show of his reluctance, and finally accepted the cash. "Bryan, we didn't invite you to stay with us expecting you to pay."

"But you got my plane ticket for me, paid for my medicine. And you've provided transportation, food, shelter. Everything."

Jeff gave him the warmest smile he'd ever seen, and as Bryan looked into his face, it nearly brought tears to Bryan's eyes. The man was everything he would ever hope to be himself, if he ever grew up. Jeff was kind and compassionate, and both he and his husband were extremely generous. They'd helped Galen and Todd, and they'd more or less adopted Trevor as their own son. Now here they were again, opening their hearts to another young person in need. Bryan didn't feel worthy.

"You're such a good kid," Jeff said. "Well, I guess I shouldn't say that. You're certainly not a kid anymore. You're a young man, and a decent one. I truly don't understand why your parents—"

"I don't care about them," Bryan interrupted. "You and Brett have been better parents to me than my parents ever have. Well, at least since I came out to them."

Jeff, who'd had his legs curled up beneath him, untucked them and sat upright on the sofa, leaning forward. "Back when I was your age, shortly after Brett and I got together, his parents all but disowned him. They were very opposed to our relationship, and they didn't want to accept that Brett was gay."

"But he came out to everyone at a sports banquet. I know the story, sir. My best friend Evan was in the play. Remember."

Jeff nodded and smiled. "Of course. But that's only part of the story. Our struggle for acceptance didn't end there just because Brett had finally decided to grow a pair and tell the whole world he was queer."

Bryan busted up laughing. It sounded funny to hear Jeff talk like that.

"That was really just the beginning. The real challenge came afterward. Brett's folks threatened to disown him, kick him out of the house, take away his car. They were very, very upset, and they sincerely believed it was their duty to do everything they could to convince their son to turn away from the homosexual *lifestyle*."

"Oh man, did they do all that stuff? Kick him out and take away his car and stuff?"

"No, they never kicked him out, and they grounded him from using the car for periods of time, but eventually they realized that Brett wasn't going to change. His mom's the one who came around first, and then his dad followed. She said she could tell just by the look in his eyes when I was around that he was madly in love with me. How could she go on condemning her son for something as pure and beautiful as being in love?"

"My mom will *never* say something like that. She thinks there is no such thing as true love when it comes to gay people. She calls it a perversion."

Jeff placed the stack of money on the coffee table in front of him and then looked up, establishing eye contact with Bryan. "Never say never, Bryan. I don't condone the way she's treated you, and I'm not making excuses for her. But we don't know what exactly is going on in her mind and in her heart. Maybe she's trying to find a way to reconcile her religious beliefs with her love for you."

Bryan didn't want to start blubbering again, but he felt tears welling in his eyes. "How can that even be a question? I thought parents were supposed to love their kids no matter what."

"I agree," Jeff said, his voice barely above a whisper. "But sometimes people do some very strange things in the name of love. She might think it's her duty to be tough with you, praying all the while you will see the light and repent."

He nodded. "Yeah, that's exactly what she thinks. I could go home tomorrow if I really wanted. All I'd have to do is tell them I'm no longer gay."

"And, of course, you can't do that. You are who you are, exactly as God created you."

"And I have a new family now."

Jeff slipped out of his seat and moved toward Bryan, extending his arms. Bryan stood and embraced him. "Yes, you do," Jeff whispered. "You're one of the family, and no matter what happens, you always will be."

CHAPTER
— 10 —

"YOU MIGHT want to consider setting up direct deposit of your payroll check," Martin said as he handed Bryan his first pay envelope.

"Yeah, I was actually gonna ask about that. I need to open up a bank account this week."

"Just bring me the routing and account numbers. There's a form we have to fill out. By the way, we're very impressed with your performance so far." Martin, who stood a couple inches shorter than Bryan, placed a hand on Bryan's shoulder. "Keep up the good work, and going forward, I'm going to start assigning you some better tables."

"Thanks, Martin. That'd be great." Bryan knew that as the new guy he often got stuck working at times when tips weren't the best and was given smaller parties to serve. Now he'd be awarded some better opportunities, which truly was good news. But it also meant he'd have to stay sharp and ultimately work even harder. "Hey, I wanted to ask you about the schedule."

"Sure," Martin said. "What's up?"

"Well, this weekend Greg's off. He's playing in a tournament."

"Yes," Martin nodded. "It's a huge event for us, and we expect to be incredibly busy."

Bryan's heart sank a bit. He'd been planning to ask if he could have Saturday off in order to watch the tournament and show his support of Greg.

"I'd love to be able to give you the weekend off, but it's just not possible." Martin answered his question before he'd even asked it. "But what I can do is schedule you early on Saturday. That way you'll be able to get out in time to make it to quarterfinals."

Bryan curled his lips into a smile. "Martin, that'd be so cool. I really appreciate it."

"Well, it's not just that Greg's off, but Ian's also requested the day off, and being down two servers, I can't even think about giving you the entire day off."

"I totally understand," Bryan said. "And to be honest, if Greg gets cut in the first elimination round, I'm not sure I'll want to be there to see that anyway."

Martin laughed. "Oh, I doubt you need to worry about that."

"You said Ian asked for the tournament off? I didn't know he played."

"Oh, he doesn't, but his boyfriend Ross is a contender. He's likely to be Greg's biggest threat."

A spike of competitive adrenaline surged through Bryan's veins. "Oh really?" He definitely wanted to be there to witness the competition. "He's that good, huh?"

"He's damn good." Martin nodded. "But I'd put my money on Greg."

"Me too," Bryan said, his voice having grown quiet. "Me too."

"YOU WANT to maintain more of a closed stance when delivering a backhand return," Greg explained.

"Whatever." Bryan wiped his brow with a towel, then draped it over his left shoulder. They were headed back inside to the locker room. "For me, this is just exercise."

"But you're improving," Greg said, his voice conveying genuine excitement.

Bryan chuckled. "Yeah, I actually scored a couple times."

"You don't get better by playing against opponents who can't beat you. You improve by challenging yourself, learning from those who play a better game than you do."

"Yeah." He nodded. "I get it, but the real reason I play against you is because I like seeing you in those shorts." He grinned as he drank in the sight of Greg's tight bubble butt and lean, muscular legs.

"You're trying to distract me with your charm," Greg teased. He stopped walking and turned around to face Bryan. "And it's working," he whispered.

Bryan stepped into Greg's personal space and placed his palm against Greg's chiseled chest. The definition was clearly visible beneath his sweat-soaked athletic shirt. "I don't think anything can distract you when you're on the court. Not even this...." He slowly snaked his fingers down Greg's torso toward his waistband.

"Mm." Greg tilted his head to the side slightly, then leaned in for a sizzling kiss.

Bryan felt something stirring in his groin, a growing appreciation of Greg's affection. And of his hot body. "Let's hit the showers," he whispered.

Bryan followed Greg the rest of the way inside the building, and with every step he took, he was aware of the throbbing inside his shorts. He held his racquet in front of him, conscious of the fact that his arousal would be obvious to anyone who happened to glance in his direction. Inside the locker room, they were alone. Thank God. Bryan froze in his tracks, a mixture of excitement and anticipation suddenly overwhelming him.

Again, Greg turned to face him, this time silently, and reached down to take hold of his own shirttail. He slowly pulled it upward, exposing his rippling six-pack. Bryan gasped, then bit his lower lip. Greg was tormenting him, literally performing a strip tease and probably knowing all the while Bryan was too timid to actually act upon his obvious arousal.

"I... uh... I thought you didn't want to risk doing anything... ya know. I thought we were gonna play it cool at work." Bryan was slightly embarrassed by the high-pitched tone of his voice. His nervousness was getting the best of him at a time when he wanted more than ever to appear cool.

"We're not at work," Greg said, with an air of insouciant bravado. "And you're jumping to conclusions. All I'm doing is getting undressed before I jump into the shower. Isn't that what we're supposed to do in a locker room?" Before Bryan could respond, Greg pulled up the shirt, further exposing his torso. The way he slowly peeled it from his chest and over his head nearly made Bryan's mouth water.

Bryan gulped. Then without even thinking about it, he reached down to grope himself. The sound that escaped his throat was unrecognizable to him.

Greg smiled. Wickedly.

Greg then toed off his shoes while simultaneously sliding his thumbs into the waistband of his shorts. His gaze remained locked on Bryan's as he slipped the shorts down past his thighs. Bryan's gaze was riveted to the noticeable bulge in Greg's white jockeys.

"Wow."

"What?" Greg's tone was innocent, as if he truly had no idea what Bryan was staring at.

Bryan wanted him. He wanted Greg so damn bad, and the more time they spent together, the more intense his desire became. This whole thing—this relationship, or whatever it was—had begun less than two weeks ago. During that period, Bryan had fantasized about intimacy with Greg many, many times, though all they'd done so far was kiss.

In his fantasies, Bryan had pleasured that body, tasted it, smelled it, kissed it. He'd made love to Greg a dozen times or more… in his dreams. And it was all he could do to hold himself back from moving a few inches closer, reaching out and touching him, taking a leap into a new level of physical intimacy.

But he couldn't do it. He shook his head and then turned away, grasping frantically for the handle of his locker.

"Bryan…." Greg moved closer, placing a hand on his shoulder. "Bryan, wait. I'm sorry…."

Bryan turned his head in order to look into Greg's eyes. He smiled, then suddenly felt more awkward than he ever had in his life. "No, it's cool," he said quietly. "Believe me, I want…."

Perhaps Greg was confused by the mixed signals Bryan was sending. Maybe he interpreted Bryan's behavior as coyness. He wrapped an arm around Bryan's torso, slid his fingers beneath the front of his shirt and gently ran them across Bryan's abdomen.

"I… uh… I do want you, ya know. I want you so fucking bad." Bryan had turned his head and was looking away from Greg. He felt Greg's bare chest pressing against his back, his bulge rubbing against Bryan's backside. "But not like this. Not here."

Bryan tilted his head to the right as Greg began to kiss his neck. The sensation sent a shiver down his spine, and he felt his own bulge growing in response. They both were sweaty, in need of showers, yet the mixture of Greg's sweat and the cologne he was wearing proved intoxicating. It was all Bryan could do to resist turning and dropping to his knees right there.

"I want it to be special… for our first time."

Slowly Greg pulled away, stepping backward a couple paces, and Bryan turned to face him again.

"You're right," Greg said. "You're totally right. I shouldn't have…."

"No, it's okay. You *should*. It's just…. Oh God!" Bryan walked over to one of the benches and sat down, then scrubbed his palms over his face. "I'm sending all the wrong signals. I want this, but then again I don't."

"You don't want *this*, or you don't want this *now*?"

"I want it! I fucking want it… I want *you*, and I want you now! But I want our first time to be something more than just a blowjob in the shower. I want it to be… special. Does that make me sound like a chick?" He was somewhat embarrassed by his admission.

Greg approached him and took a seat on the bench beside him. "No. Well, maybe a little, but it's cool. And you're right. I want it to be more than that too, and it's really not smart for us to be fooling around here."

"That's just it. I don't want it to just be fooling around. I want more than that."

"Me too." Greg pressed his lips gently against Bryan's cheek. "Meaningful and memorable."

"We still can shower together," Bryan said.

Greg rolled his eyes. "No. No, we can't."

"Huh?"

"I know if I see you naked, that'll be too much. I won't be able to control myself."

Bryan laughed and realized Greg was right.

"Saturday, after the tournament, come home with me. We'll celebrate my victory or commiserate my defeat. Either way, I want it to be with you."

"You sure?"

"Positive."

Bryan turned to him, cupped Greg's head in the palm of his hands, and kissed him deeply. "But you really need a shower," he whispered. "Bad."

"JUST CHOOSE a parking space," Trevor complained. "My God, you waste all this time driving around looking for a close parking spot, and if you'd just parked back there, we'd be inside by now."

Adam didn't seem in the least bit fazed by Trevor's complaining. "Ha-ha!" He spotted an empty spot toward the end of the aisle and sped toward it. He whipped the car into the empty space and smiled triumphantly, apparently proud of his victory.

Bryan, who was sitting in the backseat, just grinned without saying a word. The two of them were kind of cute, the way they bantered with each other. They reminded Bryan of Jeff and Brett. "So what's this meeting like? I've never been to a gay student union meeting."

"Boring," Adam said.

"It's not boring." Trevor craned his neck in order to look around the seat and make eye contact with Bryan. "But it is political sometimes. Some of the members get pretty passionate."

"Oh," Bryan said. "I'll just quietly observe."

"Sometimes they sponsor guest speakers. Politicians, gay rights activists," Adam explained. "Other times they just talk about dumb stuff like what posters they want to hang and when they wanna do the next bake sale."

"Bake sale? Who has bake sales anymore?" Bryan asked.

"Oh, don't let Dad hear you say that," Trevor cautioned. "He *loves* when we have bake sales. Last time, he made, like, twelve dozen cookies, a double batch of fudge brownies, and an enormous rainbow cake."

"I can just picture him in the kitchen." Bryan smiled. "Your dad's amazing."

The three of them got out of the car and headed toward the college entrance. They had to make their way down a long hallway to get to the conference room where the meeting was scheduled, and once inside, Bryan immediately spotted Greg.

Greg rushed over and took Bryan by the hand, then kissed him on the lips. "Thanks for coming!"

The room had been set up for the meeting with folding chairs lined up in neat rows, probably about fifty of them. But by the looks of things, they'd been a bit optimistic. There were only a few people present. Adam and Trevor took their seats in the middle, and when Greg excused himself, Bryan joined them.

"Do Todd and Galen come to this?" Bryan asked.

"Sometimes," Trevor answered, and then he began waving frantically as he caught sight of someone who'd just entered the room. "Hi, Dani!"

The girl he was waving to had short, spikey hair and looked like she weighed about eighty pounds. She smiled as Trevor jumped to his feet and rushed over to give her a hug. "Dani, this is our friend Bryan. He just moved here from Michigan."

"Hi. Nice to meet you." She extended her hand, and as Bryan reached out to shake it, she gripped his hand with an intensity unlike anything Bryan had ever felt. He squeezed her hand in response and tried not to grimace.

"Firm handshake you have there." He grinned.

Dani shrugged.

"Come on, sit with us," Trevor said.

Adam stood up and gave her a warm hug, then sat back down, one seat over, leaving an empty seat for her to sit between him and Trevor.

"Dani's on Adam's baseball team," Trevor explained.

"She is?" They had a coed baseball team here at UT?

"*He* is. Yeah," Trevor said.

"Oh… uh… sorry. I thought his name was Dani, with an i, but it's Danny with a y?"

"Right," Trevor said. "Danny's transgender. He's a catcher on the team, and he's awesome."

Before Bryan could respond, the room grew quiet as Greg stepped up to the podium. "Thanks for coming, everyone."

Bryan couldn't help but smile, seeing Greg standing up there in front of everyone. Though the room wasn't packed, there were about twenty-five students present, and Bryan felt his heart swell a bit with pride that his boyfriend was a leader. Was that what Greg was to him? His boyfriend? It was starting to feel that way, and Bryan liked it.

"We don't have an ambitious agenda tonight, just a few announcements, and then we're going to show a documentary on marriage equality. But I want to start out by welcoming some of our newcomers. Not to make anyone uncomfortable, but if this is your first meeting, if you could either raise your hand or stand, we have a welcome gift for you."

Trevor leaned over, wrapped his arm around Bryan, and pulled him to his feet. "Right here!" Trevor shouted. With his free hand he pointed in the air over Bryan's head. "This is Bryan, and this is his first meeting."

Bryan felt the heat rush to his cheeks as Greg stood there at the lectern, smiling. "Yeah, I believe we may have already made each other's acquaintance."

Adam let loose with a loud whistle, further adding to Bryan's humiliation. It felt like all eyes were on him. A female college student crossed the room, holding out a handled plastic bag. She handed it to Bryan, who accepted and thanked her, then quickly took his seat.

"Anyone else?" Greg asked.

"Right here." It was a familiar voice, and it came from the back of the room. Bryan turned around to see who it was. Ian, and he was standing next to one of the most drop-dead gorgeous guys Bryan had ever seen. "This is my friend Ross, and it's his first meeting."

"Welcome, Ross," Greg said. His greeting was sincere, which Bryan considered commendable under the circumstances. Not only was Ian a major jerk to Greg, but his boyfriend Ross was Greg's biggest competitor in his upcoming tennis tournament.

Bryan dug through his bag, checking out the contents. Mostly it contained literature, brochures that advertised local businesses and resources. There were several coupons offering student discounts and one-time-only offers, including a free pizza from a local gay-owned pizzeria and a half-off admission to the Busch Gardens theme park. Bryan recalled that Greg had mentioned taking him sometime. The packet also had a couple of magazines: one a statewide gay publication and the other a copy of the current issue of *Out*. There were also a couple of bumper stickers, one from the Human Rights Campaign and the other from the UT LGBT student union. Overall, it was a pretty cool bundle of goodies.

"It's time for us to get serious about our fall-semester fundraising event," Greg was saying. "Last year we raised over two thousand dollars from our bake sale, and we have a chance this year to again have some space at the Pride Center holiday flea market, which will be held the first weekend in December."

Several people began whispering amongst themselves, including Trevor and Adam. "Oh my God, Dad's going to go crazy if we have it at the flea market," Trevor said. "Imagine the shit he's gonna buy…."

Greg waited a few seconds for the murmuring to subside before continuing. "Now, Pride Center normally charges $350 for a table, but they've graciously offered to waive the fee. Before signing up, I wanted to get feedback, possibly vote on it."

Adam stood up and spoke confidently. "I motion we go ahead with it. We can't pass up a chance like that."

Greg nodded. "Very well. Do I hear a second to that motion?"

"I second it," came another voice from the opposite side of the room.

"Very well. All those in favor of, say 'aye.'"

Almost everyone affirmed the vote in unison.

"And those opposed...."

"I'm opposed!"

Everyone turned around at the same time to see who'd voiced the objection. Of course, it was Ian, and he was standing, posture stiff as a board and with his chin jutting out defiantly. "I think we should do something new this year, something more exciting."

This, coming from a person who lived half his life in the closet, seemed a bit shocking to Bryan. No doubt this was just another one of his attempts to create drama.

"Okay," Greg said. "And what's your proposal?"

Ian cleared his throat before continuing. "I think we should do a beefcake car wash."

Several people snickered, and Bryan glanced over to Trevor, who rolled his eyes.

"A *beefcake* car wash?" Greg asked.

"Yeah. A beefcake car wash. Ya know, hot, shirtless guys washing cars for cash. It's actually my friend Ross's idea, and he volunteers to be one of the beefcakes."

Everyone started laughing, including Bryan, as Ross pushed himself up from his seat and stood beside his boyfriend. He raised his arms into a flexing position and posed for the audience. Holy fuck, he was built like a brick shithouse.

"Can you imagine how much money we'd likely make from an event like this?"

"Wait a second," said one of the female attendees. She was sitting in the front with an all-girl group. "No offense, but some of us have zero interest in beefcake."

"Point taken," Greg said. "But who says we have to limit our fundraising to one event? Why can't we have a bake sale *and* a car wash? And why does it only have to be a beefcake car wash? We can also have a bikini babes car wash with all-female volunteers."

"Yeah!" one of the lesbians shouted. "Now you're talkin'."

"Okay, Ian has motioned for a car wash event. Do I have a second?" Greg asked.

Ross raised his hand, seconding the motion. The proposal carried, and so it seemed everyone was happy. Bryan was impressed by Greg's ability to handle everything so smoothly, defusing what could have otherwise been a contentious issue. After the announcements, when the movie began playing, Greg came over and took a seat next to Bryan, draping his arm around the back of Bryan's chair.

"You were awesome," Bryan whispered.

"I know," Greg said, and then he smiled. "Just kidding, but thanks." He kissed Bryan sweetly on the lips, and Bryan snuggled beside him to enjoy the movie.

CHAPTER
— **11** —

"BUT I feel fine," Bryan told Hank. This whole depression thing was starting to seem ridiculous. What was the point? The counseling sessions. The medications. It all could be just a racket, a way for them to make money, and lots of it. "I really don't think I need the counseling... or the pills."

"Bryan," Hank intoned, "what you're experiencing is not uncommon."

"That's my point," Bryan continued. "I wonder if my depression is just a natural part of life. We all go through rough patches. We all face situations that make us sad, and in my case, it was the rejection of my parents. But everything's changed now. I have a new family, a new relationship, and I'm doing great. I don't feel depressed anymore."

Hank nodded. "You don't feel depressed right now, and that's a good thing. But what about tomorrow? What about the day after that? What if this new relationship doesn't go exactly the way you envision? Are you ready to face all the possible challenges life seems to throw in our path? Bryan, you feel great right now because your situation has changed, and also partly because of the antidepressants. And I feel like we've been making tremendous progress with our counseling sessions."

Bryan sighed. Some people just didn't know how to take no for an answer. "Look, I can't afford this. Every single time I see you, Jeff and Brett are forking out money. Every pill I swallow is another ten bucks or more from their wallets. It'd be different if I had a way to pay for this."

"Have you considered applying for assistance?"

"Yeah, and I'm going to eventually. Jeff is helping me with that, but he said we have to wait until after the first of the year."

"Then let me make you a deal. Our remaining sessions for this year, until you get your insurance, will be pro bono. No charge."

Bryan shook his head. "I appreciate it, but what you're offering is just another handout."

"It's not a handout." Hank clasped his hands together in his lap, then closed his eyes momentarily. When he opened them, he looked directly at Bryan. "I didn't become a counselor to get rich, believe it or not. If so, I wouldn't specialize in treating LGBT youth. You're not the only young gay person who doesn't have insurance, Bryan."

"Well, then, you should be happy. I'm one less person to worry about."

Hank took a deep breath, then sighed audibly. "I can't force you to continue treatment, Bryan. But I strongly advise against discontinuing it at this stage. What you are experiencing is very typical. Patients who suffer from clinical depression often begin to feel better during treatment, when they're taking their medication and getting the services they need. They then start to feel like they've been cured, like they don't need to continue with their treatment plan. But if you quit now, I'm afraid the cycle will reset and you might have a relapse."

The cycle. What cycle?

"I don't want to be on drugs for the rest of my life," Bryan objected. "Other people go through situations far worse than I've experienced. Greg lost his dad! And he didn't need to take medication."

"Some people need to take insulin to stay alive. Others take pills for their heart or for pain management or for a number of other medical reasons. And you might be right, Bryan. This may indeed just be situational, but from our discussions, I sense it's more than that. I don't think you began battling depression as a result of your estrangement with your family. I think the situation only exacerbated a condition that was already present."

He hated feeling pressured like this. He hated the fact that this so-called treatment was such a big deal to everyone. Jeff had insisted it would help. He'd even made it conditional, part of the deal. Bryan had agreed to the counseling as one of the terms of living in Jeff and Brett's home. He probably wouldn't be happy with Bryan's decision to quit.

"Okay, but only till the end of the year. And if I can't get insurance after that, I'm definitely quitting."

"That's fair," Hank said, nodding. "I won't bill you for any of the remaining sessions this year. Of course, there's still the matter of your medication, but there's an office down at the Pride Center. They have a program that specifically provides services to the LGBT community."

"I already know about it. I'll ask Jeff."

"Good. So it's settled."

"For now."

"HOW ARE you gentlemen this afternoon?" Bryan said, greeting two men who'd just been seated in the dining room. They were obviously a couple. One had snow white hair and the other was bald. Both were dressed impeccably in the finest name-brand casual attire. "My name's Bryan, and I'll be taking care of you today."

"Oh, how nice," the bald gentlemen said. "What a treat."

Bryan smiled warmly. "Can I start you two off with something to drink?"

Older gay couples were Bryan's absolute favorite customers. They were usually cute and made a lot of comments laced with innuendo, but in truth they were perhaps the friendliest of the restaurant's clientele. They also tipped the best, and Bryan had figured out that by showing a little TLC, he could easily ratchet up that gratuity.

"Are you here for the tournament?" Bryan asked.

"Never miss it," the white-haired gentleman said. "We love to watch, don't we, Gerald?"

"It's the highlight of the fall season. The grace and athletic beauty of those young athletes… it all just makes me wax nostalgic."

"Yes, sir. I know exactly what you mean. I hope to make it over to the courts in time for the quarterfinals. I have a *very* close friend who's a contender."

"Ohhh? Do tell." The white-haired gentleman leaned forward, intently hanging on every word.

"Well, his name's Greg, and he also works here."

"Have you been, how shall I say, *interested* in this young man for long?" Gerald inquired.

"A few weeks." Bryan nodded and smiled. He then lowered himself, crouching down at the side of the table between the two men. "Tonight we're having a very special, celebratory sleepover, if you know what I mean," he whispered.

The white-haired gentleman clapped his hands together. "Oh, that's wonderful! We'll be in the stands, and we'll watch for you. What is this other boy's name again?"

"Greg Lewis. He'll be easy to spot. He's the good-looking one."

They both laughed. "Oh, thank you for that clarification. Obviously you're a well-suited couple, then."

"Aw, that's sweet of you to say." He offered his warmest smile, making eye contact with each of them. "Have you decided on a beverage? An appetizer, maybe, to start things off?"

"I don't know about an appetizer, but I sure do know what I want for dessert!" Gerald joked.

Bryan laughed. "You're a tease, aren't you?"

"Now that's the pot calling the kettle black."

When the couple left forty minutes later, Bryan could barely contain his excitement. He'd just received his first hundred-dollar tip. "Hell yeah!" he said, pumping his fist in the air.

Traci happened to be walking by the register where Bryan was standing. "What're you all psyched about?"

"Just got an awesome tip," Bryan said. "A hundred bucks."

"Let me guess. It was from that older couple you just had at table fourteen."

"Exactly. How'd you know?"

"I could see the way they were flirting with you. You gay guys are shameless, ya know."

"Fuck that," he said, lowering his voice. He was still smiling. "As if you don't pour on the charm for a nice tip."

"Believe me, I try, but most straight guys are cheap. Either that, or they're perverts. I've never seen a gay customer get grab-assy with one of the waiters. If anything, they're even nicer. But when it's an older straight guy who's got the hots for a young waitress, he ends up being a dirty old man."

"What can I say? Gay men are just nicer in general."

"Ha! Maybe, but what about creeps like Ian? Imagine what he'll be like when he gets older."

"If he lives that long," Bryan said.

IT WAS almost five when Bryan finally got out of work. Greg had already texted him, telling him he'd made it through eliminations and quarterfinals and was moving on to semifinals. That meant only four players remained in the competition. Bryan hurried across the parking lot toward the courts, hoping to get there before the end of the match.

Trevor and Adam were waiting for him when he arrived, and Bryan made his way to join them in the stands. He looked down at the court, and the first thing he saw was the backside of Greg, sexy as hell.

"The score is 40-15. Greg needs one more point to win the set and match."

Bryan was still trying to make sense of the scoring, but he understood games were played until one player won four points. Each set consisted of six games. There were three sets in the match. The first player to win two sets won the match.

"What about Ross?" Bryan asked.

"He won his match already. If Greg wins here, they'll play each other."

"Fuck," Bryan whispered.

"No shit. Ross is good. He kicked ass all day today, but then so did Greg."

Just then the crowd erupted into applause. "Game, set, match," the announcer declared. Greg raised his hands into the air, holding his racquet high above his head, and tossed his head back. Damn if he didn't look like the sexiest man on earth. Bryan leapt to his feet and began cheering.

"There'll be, like, a twenty-minute break," Trevor said.

"Let's go see Greg!"

As soon as Greg spotted Bryan, he rushed across the court and scooped him up into his arms, embracing him fiercely. "Oh my God! I made it to finals."

"I got here just in time to see the final point."

"Did you hear who I'm playing against?" He'd set Bryan down, but still had both his hands on Bryan's shoulders.

"I know, Trevor told me it's Ross."

"He's notorious for cheating." Greg lowered his voice and steered Bryan over to the back of the court, out of earshot of anyone nearby.

"How? I didn't think it was possible in a tournament."

"Yeah, it's a lot more difficult. In junior tournaments it happens all the time because there aren't enough judges to go around. Cheaters like Ross will hook ya every chance they can." Bryan had no idea what that even meant.

"But he can't cheat here?"

"Not really. He tries, though. I saw him when he was playing earlier. He talks really loudly, shouts things out as his opponent is preparing to serve." That just seemed childish to Bryan, but then when he considered how players fouled each other in basketball, it wasn't surprising.

"And that's legal?"

"Not technically, but people get away with it. I don't care, because I'm not about to let his big mouth break my concentration or interfere with my game." He leaned over and picked up a bottle of water, then took a swig.

"I can't believe you've been playing all day."

"Yeah, but I'm glad we have time to finish. It would suck if this extended to tomorrow. I'm pumped right now, man. I'm so close to victory, I can almost taste it."

Bryan fully related to what Greg was saying. The year his basketball team had won the state championship, victory was the only thing that had mattered. The entire team had pushed themselves to a point of exhaustion, and nobody even noticed till it was over.

"I'm here for ya," Bryan said.

"I know you are… and thanks." Bryan thought for a second Greg was about to lean in and kiss him. Instead he smiled and rubbed Bryan's back.

"I made a buttload in tips," Bryan said. "So no matter what happens, dinner's my treat."

"What do you mean, no matter what happens?" He offered a cocky grin.

"Oh, right. I mean, after you win!"

"That's better."

"I better go. I'll be in the stands cheering you on."

Greg smiled and winked, and Bryan sensed he wanted to say something more, but he turned away.

BRYAN KNEW what it was like to train hard for a sport. His coach back in Boyne City had been a demanding bastard, pushing his teammates and him to accomplish goals they themselves hadn't even yet imagined. They'd practiced daily, often early in the morning or late at night. As a result, their team succeeded, and they won the championship.

Tennis was different. It wasn't a team sport, and though Greg had benefited from the tutelage of a coach, everything he'd accomplished was a result of his own hard work. Previously Bryan had mocked the sport, thinking it wasn't even in the same category as real sports like basketball and football. But now he knew better.

Bryan wondered if he'd have had the stamina to compete in a tournament like this. Greg had been on the court, playing since early that morning, and it all had built up to this grand finale. One more match, and then it would be over. Win or lose, Greg would then start the process again, training for his next tournament. Sure, there'd be prize money. There would be a trophy and some press coverage. Greg would have his moment in the spotlight, even if he only finished in second place. But he wouldn't have a team to celebrate with. The joy of his victory or the crushing agony of his defeat would be solitary emotions.

And it suddenly struck Bryan that Greg didn't seem to have any family there supporting him. He'd told Bryan that his mom was accepting and supportive. He'd mentioned he had an older sister. So where were they?

As the announcer introduced the players, Greg and Ross took their positions on the court. Bryan was struck by the fact that Greg, though still the hottest man on the planet, looked as if he'd just run a marathon. He was wearing a headband, and his golden hair appeared much darker than its natural color, now damp with sweat. His shirt was drenched and clung to his sweat-soaked torso, revealing his toned, chiseled physique. Bryan hadn't realized how powerful and muscular Greg's legs were, and as he assumed a stance, ready to receive the first serve, the fabric of his white shorts pulled tightly across his buttocks. Bryan felt pretty warm himself as he took in the sight, and he reached up to wipe his brow.

Ross, on the other hand, looked as if he'd just stepped out of *GQ Magazine*. He was tall, like Greg, though not quite as muscular. He possessed darker features, jet-black hair and chocolate-colored eyes. If Bryan hadn't known either of them, it would've been difficult to decide who was better looking.

He wondered what about himself had attracted Greg. Bryan had never hated his own appearance. He realized he was an okay-looking guy. He was in shape, had a nice smile, a decent height. But, God, Greg could have any guy he wanted.

Greg had explained to Bryan that he was a baseliner, which meant he generally positioned himself near the back of the court. Baseliners were aggressive players, highly energetic, because they had to rush forward when necessary. It appeared Ross employed the same tactic. The two were evenly matched, and as the first game began, this was reflected in the score. Greg was running his ass off, fighting for every point, but so was his opponent.

The first game went to Ross, and Bryan's heart sank. It was difficult for him to sit quietly in the stands. In basketball the spectators were far more active, cheering at every point, booing the umpires for bad calls, and charged with kinetic, contagious enthusiasm. Tennis was so different. There were "oohs" and "ahhs" and polite applause, but Bryan didn't think these fans were the type to bust out a tailgate party in the parking lot.

During the second game, Greg rallied and tied the set. He was making his comeback. And from that point forward, he seemed to have renewed energy, bolstered by his win. The momentum carried, and Greg went on to win the set, but then Ross fought his way back and tied it up with the second set.

"Fuck," Bryan whispered to Trevor. "This match is aggravating. It's got me on pins and needles."

"Still think it's a pussy sport?"

Bryan playfully slugged Trevor's puny bicep. "All right, I admit it. I w-w-wuh-was...."

"Wrong!" Trevor finished for him. "It's so refreshing to hear you admit that." He really was cute when he acted smug like that.

"How do you put up with this?" Bryan asked Adam.

"Don't even get me started."

"Look at where Ian is," Trevor said, ignoring them. "How the hell did he get a courtside seat like that?"

Bryan looked down at the court and spotted him. "Isn't that where the coaches sit?"

"Yeah, and he sure as hell isn't a tennis coach. I wonder if that's at all distracting to Greg."

"It doesn't seem to be," Bryan said. "Greg's pretty focused. It's weird, though, that Ross doesn't even seem to break a sweat. Look at how unfazed he is, even though he's running his butt off. And Greg's sweating like a pig."

Trevor shrugged. "Maybe that's why some people really do think it's a pussy sport. Some players just seem too composed. I don't get it, really."

As play resumed, Ross became more animated. He started reacting to every point, pumping his fist in the air each time he scored. Greg didn't seem to be bothered and continued to focus on his game.

Again Greg rallied and tied it up with the fourth game. The winner had to win by two points in order to win the set, so Greg would have to win the next two games in order to avoid a tiebreaker. Greg won the first game and needed to only win one more for it to be game, set, and match. He'd be the tournament champion.

The score was 40-15, the same situation as with the semifinals, and Greg only needed one more point. He was now on the opposite side of the court from where Bryan was sitting, and Bryan could see the determination in his face.

"Come on," Bryan whispered, "you can do this."

As Greg raised his racquet, preparing to serve, he suddenly froze, then stepped briskly to the side of the court. His facial features warped into an expression of anger and frustration. He started yelling, pointing his finger at someone. An official quickly made his way out onto the court as a murmur rose in the stands.

"What's going on?" Bryan said, now on his feet.

"It's that fucking Ian," Trevor said. "He said something to Greg that pissed him off, and he's going ballistic."

Bryan looked down at the court and saw Ross standing calmly on his side of the net. As Ross turned around, Bryan noticed the grin on his face. "You fucker," Bryan said under his breath. "I hope Greg kicks your ass."

A few seconds later, Ian was escorted off the court by two officials, and Bryan wondered what exactly he'd done that had gotten to Greg. He prayed it didn't interfere with the outcome of the match. Greg resumed his position and tossed the ball in the air, then delivered a forceful serve.

Ross returned the serve and the ball volleyed back and forth across the court. Finally, as Bryan held his breath, Greg seized the opportunity, using an overhead smash to plant the ball just out of reach of his opponent. The spectators jumped to their feet, cheering wildly.

"Holy shit," Bryan said, grabbing Trevor and hugging him tightly. "He did it! He won!" He then turned to Adam and embraced him as well.

Greg was at the center of the court, shaking hands with Ross, who at last no longer had that cocky grin smeared across his face. Bryan wondered what exactly they were saying to each other as they pumped each other's hand furiously.

CHAPTER
— **12** —

BRYAN WAS giddy with excitement as he climbed into the car with Greg. It had taken another two hours after the match concluded for them to finally make their way off the court and into the locker room. First, there had been the awards presentation, then Greg had to pose for photos. People kept coming up to congratulate him, and he took time to greet each one. Bryan waited patiently, even after Trevor and Adam departed.

"You were amazing," Bryan said as he slid into the passenger seat.

Greg, who was now freshly showered and changed, smiled at him warmly. "Thanks. I'm so stoked right now!" He grabbed hold of Bryan by the shoulders and pulled him in for a kiss, deep and passionate.

"Mm. Do you have any idea how sexy you were out there on the court?"

Greg laughed. "I was a big ball of nasty, stinky sweat… kind of the opposite of sexy."

"I dunno. I think you looked hot. I don't mind your mansweat."

"Well, we both had good days, and you're looking pretty damn sexy yourself right now."

Bryan was flattered and leaned in to kiss him again, but only briefly. "I was thinking about that," he said, "and I wonder, what exactly is it about me that a guy like you even finds attractive?"

"Please don't do that," Greg said. His voice contained no venom, only warmth and sincerity. "I know it's not your fault, but it hurts me."

Confused, Bryan pulled back. "What do you mean?"

"When you put yourself down."

"But I didn't. I just asked…."

"Bryan, I could list a dozen or more things about you that I think are amazing. And you know what? I will. I'll do exactly that. I'll tell you every day how gorgeous you are, how intelligent and witty and charming, how your heart of gold is so touching to me. I'll tell you all those things because they're true. But I wish you could get to a point where you can start telling them to yourself."

"I didn't mean…."

"I know you weren't fishing for compliments. Believe me, I get it. I understand that you have insecurities, that you doubt yourself constantly. If only you could see yourself the way I do, you'd realize how lovable you are. Bryan, this is the first time since I was fourteen that anyone has shown up to root for me at a tournament."

Bryan felt like such a loser at that moment. He'd somehow managed to make the conversation about himself when they should have been celebrating Greg's big victory. "I'm sorry," he whispered. "You're so popular, though. I thought you'd have a zillion people there cheering for you."

"Oh, I do. I do have fans and supporters, and that's not what I mean. I mean someone special. Family. Loved ones."

Bryan again wondered why this was the case. Greg had said his mom was loving and supportive, so why wasn't she there? "What about your mom?"

Greg fastened his seat belt and engaged the ignition. "Um, well, can I explain all that when we get back to my place? How 'bout we pick up some takeout? I'm about starving right now."

"You don't want to go out to a nice restaurant?"

Greg made a face. "Uh, not really. I just want to be with you. Quality time, ya know."

"Sounds perfect." Bryan took Greg's hand in his own and gave it a gentle squeeze as they pulled out of the parking lot.

GREG'S HOME wasn't impressive the way Jeff and Brett's was, but it was nice. It was a split-level ranch in a decent neighborhood. He had a two-car garage and a decent yard and what appeared to be a perfectly manicured lawn.

"You live here alone?" Bryan asked as he followed Greg inside.

"I do… at least for now. This is my mom's house, actually." Greg was holding the enormous trophy he'd won in one hand and the take-out bag in the other.

Bryan looked around. There had been no other cars in the garage, and the living room was empty. "It's her house, but she doesn't live here?"

Greg led the way through the living room and into the small dining room, where he placed the bag on the table. Burgers and fries again. They were Greg's favorite. "Oh my God, I'm so hungry." He pulled out a chair for Bryan, then took a seat next to him.

"Thanks," Bryan said.

Greg set the trophy he was carrying on the buffet, then unpacked the bag and placed Bryan's food in front of him on the table. He then took a sip from his Coke and set it down on the table. "My mom's not here," he said. "She's in a hospital. Well, it's kind of a hospital. It's actually more like a group home."

"I'm sorry." It wasn't what Bryan had expected to hear. "I had no idea."

"After my dad died, she sort of had a breakdown. She has periods where she does really well, and then she relapses. The last time she was hospitalized, her doctor suggested this facility. It's kind of a halfway house, I guess. She really likes it there, and she's doing well."

"Why can't she come home?"

"Oh, she can, and hopefully she will soon. But the important thing right now is that she's in a safe environment. It wasn't the easiest decision, but she's the one who made it. She's so unselfish." He stuffed a fry in his mouth, then took another sip of his drink. "She refused to let me quit school to take care of her."

"Oh, Greg…."

"It's okay. Really. And like I told you already, she's really supportive of me. It's just, after Dad passed away, she couldn't come to my tournaments anymore. It was just too hard on her."

Bryan wanted to know more. He wanted to ask specific questions about her condition, but he didn't want to pry. Obviously she was suffering from a type of mental illness.

"Mom was always very fragile." Greg continued, almost as if he were speaking to himself, his voice quiet. The intonation was soothing, in spite of the gravity of his words. "She'd battled severe depression most of her life, and I think my dad was kind of like a stabilizer to her. He was her rock. Her security. When he died, she fell apart."

Bryan didn't speak, simply because he had no words. Instead, he placed his hand atop Greg's and offered a weak but sincere smile.

"There've been four suicide attempts. Seven 'severe depressive episodes' altogether. She's been in the psych ward a dozen times, has had ECT."

"ECT?"

"Electroconvulsive therapy. Sometimes it's very effective in treating severe depression, but it often results in memory loss. In her case, she's lost a lot of memories, but she hasn't forgotten the essential things. She knows her kids, just doesn't remember everything we've been through. Really, that's not such a bad thing…."

Oh God. Bryan couldn't imagine.

"I'm sorry I didn't tell you any of this earlier."

"No, it's okay. I totally understand."

"It's just I had a bad experience. It was with Ian, actually."

"Fuck Ian. I'm really starting to despise that asshole. What'd he say to you tonight on the court that got you so pissed?"

"Well, he shouldn't have even been there, courtside, and it was my own fault. I should have protested earlier. He was running his mouth, nonstop, trying to distract me."

"I'm glad you got him kicked out."

"Not exactly kicked out, but I asked them to remove him from courtside seat. That section is reserved for coaches."

"What'd he say to you?"

"Started yelling shit about my crazy mother."

"That bastard." Bryan felt fury boiling inside him. If Ian were there, he knew he'd pulverize him.

"Ian's just a jerk. He plays dirty, and I should have known better than to let him bait me. It could have cost me the match. Fortunately, this time it had the opposite effect. He ended up pissing me off and I ass-whupped his boyfriend. Figuratively speaking, of course."

Bryan laughed. "That you did, and it was fucking awesome!"

"Anyway, when I started seeing Ian, it was right after Mom had suffered an episode. I was sort of vulnerable at the time, and I opened up to him, told him about the situation. He wasn't exactly understanding, and I knew he wasn't the right guy for me."

"He's not," Bryan agreed. "And not just because he was a jerk about your mom. He doesn't deserve a guy as awesome as you."

Greg smiled. "Thanks. Well, he has Ross now, and hopefully he'll be happier and stop doing mean shit to other people."

"I wouldn't count on it."

"Let's not worry about Ian tonight. Okay? He's not worth our energy."

"Agreed."

"So you live here alone, then?"

"My sister's married and lives in Denver. She visits when she can. Her name's Jenny. But other than when she visits, I'll be here alone until my mom is released. And I'm starting to think she might be better off where she's at. She loves it there, and I get to see her whenever I want. Sometime I'd like to take you to meet her."

"I'd love that."

When Greg looked at Bryan, there were tears in Greg's eyes. He took hold of Bryan's hand and held it, making no advances, simply sharing the warmth of his touch. "I somehow believed I could trust you, Bryan. I just knew you'd understand."

"Of course, I understand." Bryan shifted himself in his chair and extended his arm, wrapping it around Greg's shoulder.

Greg leaned into him, pulling Bryan into a tight embrace. "Thank you," he whispered. "I love you so much."

BRYAN WASN'T a virgin. Not only had he been intimate with Liam, but he'd also experimented with a couple other guys. His feelings for Liam were the closest he'd ever come to the L word. And yes, he'd said it. He'd told Liam he loved him, and Liam had responded reciprocally.

But had that really been love?

Bryan had learned a lot about love growing up. In his family and church, the word was used frequently. God loved him. His parents and family loved him. He loved them. But the one context in which "love" was not frequently used in his childhood household was in the romantic sense.

True love, he'd been taught, was spiritual. The Greek word agape described a type of love, from God, that was unconditional. It was the purest, truest type of love that transcended all human emotion. This love, he'd been taught, was the love of Christ. It was a love so strong and comprehensive that Jesus had willingly laid down his life for the world.

Bryan didn't believe in that kind of love. Not anymore. For all those years he'd been taught that the love of God was the only real love, and that homosexuals were incapable of experiencing it. They were driven by lust and perversion, and their relationships made a mockery of God's love. They'd given themselves over to a lie, had exchanged that which was true and pure for something corrupt and sinister.

Yeah, he really had been taught all that bullshit.

And he no longer believed it. Back in Michigan, after his parents kicked him out of the house, he'd made a conscious decision *not* to believe. How could he believe in something that was supposedly unconditional that had such uncompromising prerequisites? God would love him unconditionally, but only if he denied his feelings and lived a life that was contrary to his very nature, a nature that God himself had created.

It made no sense. But what did make sense to Bryan was the relationship Jeff and Brett shared. If there was anything Bryan could associate with true love, it was that connection. Not only did they obviously love each other, but their very affects seemed to radiate love for those around them, the significant people in their lives. Adam and his sister Lisa were loved, incontrovertibly. And the whole family put their love into action, helping those in need, providing support and resources, and simply being amazing Good Samaritans.

To Bryan, these people represented love in a manner that starkly contrasted with his family and his church. And now Greg was a part of this equation.

He did love his new family. He loved Jeff, Brett, Adam, Trevor, and Lisa more than he'd ever thought possible. And as he opened himself to Greg and bared his soul, he was beginning to develop a trust he'd never known with Liam. His respect and admiration for Greg had also grown exponentially.

The pain and hardship Greg had endured in his life—first having lost his father at the age of thirteen, then supporting his mom as she battled severe mental health issues—Bryan's heart bled for him. And this picture, this broader, more expansive portrait of the real Greg, was very different from the person Bryan had initially assumed him to be. Greg was not a rich spoiled brat who hung out at the country club.

He was a member of the country club so that he could pursue his passion, which was tennis. But he worked hard to pay his membership fees. He donated his time at the Pride Center and served as president of the LGBT student union. He was loved and respected by almost everyone who knew him.

And Bryan's feelings for Greg were deeper than anything he'd experienced before. Though he had yet to touch him intimately, at least in the physical sense, he felt closer to Greg than he ever had to Liam.

So why couldn't he say the words? When Greg told Bryan he loved him, why couldn't he utter a reciprocal reply?

Greg hadn't pressed him. Obviously he wasn't expecting quid pro quo. He was merely expressing his genuine feelings. He loved Bryan, plain and simple.

They embraced, and Bryan held him. Tonight was their celebration, or it was supposed to be. They were supposed to be rejoicing in Greg's victory. Another trophy. A big chunk of prize money.

Instead, Greg had opened his heart and bared his soul. He'd allowed Bryan to see his vulnerabilities. And for the first time since Bryan had stepped foot on Florida soil, he didn't feel so much like a victim. He held Greg tightly and lent his strength, and it felt damn good.

"Will you come to my room with me?" Greg whispered. He pulled back and looked Bryan in the eye. Tears were streaming down Greg's cheeks.

Bryan nodded.

Greg took him by the hand and led him up the short flight of steps into his room. He turned on a lamp, and the subdued lighting cast an ambiance on the room that set the mood. Bryan stepped over to the bed and waited, watching Greg as he crossed the room toward him.

"You're beautiful," Greg said, and then he kissed him again. The passion of Greg's kiss stirred something deep within Bryan, and he responded. He wrapped his arms around Greg, caressing his back, working his way upward to his shoulders. Bryan felt Greg pressing against him, rubbing their pelvises together, giving rise to a yearning within Bryan—a throbbing that begged for release.

Greg put his hands on the sides of Bryan's face, framing it as he continued to kiss him passionately. Bryan opened his mouth, receiving Greg, feeling his tongue as it probed, and Bryan responded in kind. Greg moved his hands downward, gliding gently across Bryan's shoulders before snaking them down his torso. Down further, slowly, he softly traced the sensitive sides of Bryan's abdomen with his fingertips. Bryan moaned and slid his hand beneath Greg's shirttail, making contact with the smooth skin of Greg's back.

Bryan's shirt was being lifted over his head as Greg briefly broke from the kiss. Greg tossed it carelessly behind him, then peeled off his own shirt. They immediately began exploring each other, fingers and tongues worshiping the other's body. And before he knew it, Bryan was on his back, lying on the mattress, with Greg leaning over him. Greg's body pressed against him as they continued to kiss and grope each other. Bryan used his hands to explore Greg's perfect physique, memorizing every detail.

"Can I take off your pants?" Greg whispered. He was staring into Bryan's eyes, and Bryan was lost in that amazing sea of blue. He nodded, and Greg reached down to slowly unbutton Bryan's khakis, then unzipped them. His heart raced a little faster as Greg peeled open Bryan's fly, then slowly slipped his khakis down past his shins and finally removed them altogether.

Bryan was throbbing with anticipation as he looked up into Greg's eyes. He'd fantasized about this moment, imagined many times how it would be, and now at last the time had come. His heartbeat quickened, and as Greg leaned in to kiss him once more, a rush of adrenaline surged through Bryan. He grabbed Greg by the shoulders and spun him around, exchanging positions with him so that now Greg lay on his back while Bryan pinned him beneath his body.

Bryan closed his eyes as their mouths connected once more, and the fervency of his kiss demanded a response. Greg returned the kiss, moaning ever so softly—gasping, tasting, probing Bryan's mouth with his tongue.

Frantically, Bryan grasped with both hands, reaching for the fly of Greg's jeans. He couldn't seem to tear off his clothes rapidly enough, but at last, with a little assistance from Greg, he had the package opened. He slid his palm inside, rubbing the bulge with his palm. Greg reflexively bucked his hips, thrusting his pelvis upward as he moaned. Bryan kissed him even more passionately.

Finally he pulled back and quickly slid off the mattress, dropping to his knees beside the bed. He reached up and grabbed hold of the waistbands of Greg's jeans and underwear and tugged them down simultaneously. Greg offered no objection, assisting by rising slightly from the mattress.

Bryan couldn't wait any longer. As much as he wanted to extend the foreplay, he needed to have all of Greg. He needed him *now*. With pants and underwear discarded, Greg lay before him completely exposed. And, God, was he beautiful. Bryan took hold of him, wrapped his thumb and forefinger around the base of Greg's shaft, and pulled it toward him. He opened his mouth and dove for it, impaling himself with Greg's hardness, swallowing the entirety in one smooth movement.

Greg cried out, then moaned loudly. "Oh fuck! Bryan... God, yes!"

Using his tongue and throat, Bryan at first applied intense suction, then gradually backed off, sucking all the while until his lips made their way up to the crown. Then he eased his way back down, nice and slow.

This wasn't his first picnic. He knew how to pleasure another man, and he wanted nothing more than to give Greg the best blowjob of his life. As he continued to suck, Bryan began to pick up the pace, bobbing on Greg's slick shaft. He used his hand as well, stroking the shaft in conjunction with his mouth as it slid up and down, faster and faster.

"Oh baby, that feels so good."

Bryan paused and looked up, making eye contact. Though his mouth was full, he hoped he was smiling with his eyes. Greg grinned as he looked down at him, then reached out to stroke the sides of Bryan's face. He ran his fingers through Bryan's short hair as Bryan slid back down the shaft and resumed his ministrations.

Having showered prior to leaving the country club, Greg smelled clean, with only a hint of musk. He tasted exactly like Bryan had imagined he would, and Bryan savored the manly scent and taste, eagerly devouring him. With his free hand, he slipped a finger into the crack of Greg's buttocks, probing for his hole.

Greg spread his legs further apart, welcoming him. "Ahhh," he moaned, as Bryan gained entrance.

He continued to slide up and down Greg's cock, sucking and stroking while he slid his finger deeper inside. He felt Greg's cock throb harder against his tongue as he pistoned his digit deep into the tight hole.

"Oh God, Bryan! I'm gonna shoot! I can't... I can't hold back. Oh God! Ahhh! Yes!"

Bryan pulled back just as Greg crossed the point of no return and volleys of cum erupted from his cockhead. Copious ropes of creamy fluid sprayed Bryan's face as he tilted his head back and eagerly received the facial. He continued to stroke, milking out every little drop.

Greg was trembling when Bryan slid back onto the mattress beside him. He grabbed hold of Bryan and pulled him in, kissing him passionately and tasting his own cum.

BRYAN FELT Greg's arousal pressing against him as Greg continued to kiss him. He was still rock hard. Greg had his hands all over him, caressing his chest and pinching his sensitive nipples. And his lips, now wet and sticky, found Bryan's neck. Bryan moaned and writhed on the mattress as Greg pinned his body to the bed.

"I want you inside me," Greg whispered. "I want you so bad!"

Those weren't the words Bryan had expected to hear, but his cock seemed to love what it was hearing. It throbbed in his tight boxer briefs, begging for release.

"Oh baby, yes," Bryan whispered.

Greg grabbed hold of Bryan's waistband and hastily stripped off his underwear, then stumbled awkwardly away from the bed. He steadied himself by grabbing hold of the nightstand, then pulled open the top drawer and removed a tube of lube and a condom.

Bryan smiled as he reached down to stroke himself.

"You were prepared."

"Always."

Greg sat down on the mattress beside him, then leaned over and took Bryan into his mouth. Bryan closed his eyes as he felt the warmth encircle him. He moaned.

"I didn't take you for a bottom," Bryan whispered when Greg released him and sat up. He looked down at Bryan's face.

"Versatile," he said, and then he winked.

"Fucking perfect."

Greg already had the edge of the condom packet between his teeth. He tore it open and removed the condom as Bryan held his pole upright, waiting for it to be sheathed. Greg positioned the condom and rolled it down around his shaft, nice and snug. He then applied the lube.

Straddling him, Greg climbed onto the mattress. His knees were on either side of Bryan's body as he lowered himself, reaching behind to guide Bryan into his hole. He moaned as the tip initially penetrated.

It was all Bryan could do not to buck his hips and drive himself in further. But he allowed Greg to maintain control. Slowly he eased himself down, and the heat that began to surround Bryan's hard-on was heavenly. "Oh God, you're so tight."

"And you're so big... shit."

"You okay, babe?" Bryan asked. He reached up to caress Greg's pectorals, then gently tweaked his nipples.

"Oh yeah... more than okay." He impaled himself further. As he slid all the way down Bryan's shaft, Greg's own cock rose to attention. Bryan took hold of it and began to stroke.

"Ahhh," Greg moaned. He grabbed hold of Bryan's shoulders as he used his legs to push himself upward, then slid back down. He was using Bryan to fuck himself. Riding his cock.

Bryan responded by thrusting, coordinating his movements to the rocking motion of Greg's body. A perfect rhythm. The tight hot hole stroked Bryan's rigid shaft, bringing him closer and closer to heavenly release. At last he couldn't hold back any longer. He moaned and cried out, "Greg, I'm gonna cum! Oh fuck yeah!"

Greg leaned forward, kissing him passionately as he felt the snap and erupted into the condom, firing his load deep inside Greg's tight, warm hole. He wrapped his arms tightly around Greg's torso, bucking his hips as he kissed and moaned simultaneously.

He was gasping, trying to catch his breath as Greg finally pulled back from the kiss. He looked up into Greg's face, which was now twisted in orgasmic pleasure. Bryan grabbed hold of Greg's shaft and pumped it, just in time to pull out another blast of spunk.

Greg moaned and bounced several times on Bryan's still-hard cock. "Oh fuck!"

This was by far the hottest sexual experience of Bryan's life. His head dropped back on the mattress as he closed his eyes and sighed. "I love you too."

CHAPTER
— **13** —

BRYAN AWAKENED in a strange bed. Alone. And then he remembered.

They'd made love, he and Greg, and it had been amazing. Beautiful. Then Greg had retrieved a pint of mint chocolate chip ice cream from the kitchen, along with two spoons, and they'd shared it while sitting cross-legged on the bed.

Greg told Bryan about the photos in his room. Some were posters, some framed pictures. All were of pro tennis players. An athlete about Greg's age, with the same caramel-colored hair, adorned the wall opposite the bed. Stefan Edberg, when he was young, Greg had explained. Bryan had no idea who he was.

"He's the greatest tennis player of all time... in my opinion." Bryan sensed he was a role model to Greg, his hero. "But I don't want to be a pro tennis player. Not anymore."

"You're good, though. You just won a tournament!"

"I entered the tournament because it was here. Playing professionally would require me to tour, and that's not an option."

"Why not play on the college team? You could get a scholarship."

He shoveled a big spoonful of ice cream into his mouth, savored the minty taste, then swallowed as he shook his head. "For the past six weeks, I've trained six hours a day. Three hours of physical training every morning. The gym, running, cardiovascular." His body evidenced his claims. "And of course there's time spent on the court hitting the ball, but the most important component is mental. Concentration."

"What do you do for that?"

"Meditation and tai chi."

"As in martial arts?"

"At least two hours a day."

Bryan couldn't believe Greg had time for all that, what with his work schedule, school, and his role in the LGBT Student Union. "You're like Superman. How do you have time?"

"I don't, and I'm glad the tournament is over. Playing on the college team would have been impossible. They want... no, they *demand*... 110 percent. And I'm disqualified, even if I wanted to. I'm considered pro because of the prize money."

"I don't get it." Bryan gently ran his fingertips up the length of Greg's forearm. "You said you don't wanna play pro."

"I hardly have time to see my mom as it is. At least now that this tournament is behind me, I can focus on getting her home."

His words seemed to contradict what he'd said earlier, that she was happy in the group home and might stay there indefinitely. "That's your goal? Bringing her home."

He looked Bryan in the eye and nodded. "Of course."

"You're a good son. You're an *amazing* son, I mean. She's lucky...."

"Don't say that. She's been through so much."

"I didn't mean—"

"No, I know what you meant." He leaned forward and gave a Bryan a sweet, chocolatey kiss. "I play tennis because I love the game. It's fun, and that's what every sport should be."

Bryan wished he could agree, but remembered a time when basketball was everything to him, much more than just a game. It had its moments where it was fun, but it was a whole hell of a lot of hard work too.

"I love it because there's a time when I'm playing where I lose myself. It's like I become one with the racquet, and it's all about the game. It's about connecting with the ball. They call that being in the zone."

"Were you in the zone tonight?"

He smiled. "I was a few minutes ago, with you."

Bryan grinned, his cheeks aflame. "I meant earlier, on the court."

"I was," he said, nodding, "but not until that last set. Ross was starting to shake my confidence. His attitude, so cocky and unconcerned. But he started to lose it right around the time Ian was escorted from the court."

"What do you think about when you're in the zone?"

"The ball, connecting with it. I don't think about strategy or how much I want to win. I don't think about my mom or my job or any of the pressures of life. I'm just lost in the game."

"I think I get it."

"No more tournaments this year. No more six-hour daily workouts. Even if I hadn't won today, I'd decided I had to refocus. I need to hit the books, concentrate on my education."

"Have you even chosen a major?"

"Premed," he said confidently. "I'm going into mental health. I want to be a psychologist."

As Bryan lay there, recalling the conversation, a chill traveled down his spine. What the two of them had shared had all seemed so perfect. But did Bryan want a relationship with a guy whose life ambition was to become a shrink? It would be like dating Hank.

His mind raced as he remembered the intimate conversations they'd shared. Greg had proven himself as a friend, a good listener. In fact, he always seemed to know exactly what to say. He seemed to understand Bryan and all he was experiencing and feeling. Was this because Greg was analyzing him? Did Greg really love him, or did he view Bryan as a case study?

No, last night had been special. The intimacy they'd shared had cemented their connection, and it was Greg who'd opened up to Bryan. He'd poured out his soul, revealed a side of himself Bryan hadn't previously known. Bryan pushed his doubts back as he snuggled under the covers.

"Morning."

Bryan rubbed his eyes with the back of his hand and looked up to see his handsome stud pushing the bedroom door open. He was carrying a fast-food take-out bag. "Brought you breakfast," Greg said.

"Mm. I want *you* for breakfast."

Greg laughed as he set the bag and beverage cups on the bedside stand. "I can be your appetizer."

"Yum." Bryan looked into his eyes and smiled. "Come here." He held out his arms and pulled Greg down to him, kissing him deeply, in spite of the morning breath he feared he had. Greg didn't seem to notice.

"I got you a breakfast sandwich," Greg said when he pulled back from the kiss. He sat on the edge of the mattress and picked up the bag, unpacking it. "Just did an eight-mile run, and now I'm about to cancel out all that hard work with an Egg McMuffin."

"I don't think you have anything to worry about. Why didn't you wake me? I'd have run with you."

"You looked so peaceful. You're cute when you're sleeping." He leaned forward and kissed Bryan's forehead.

Bryan pushed himself upright and propped a pillow behind his back. "You're all hot and sweaty now."

Greg made a face. "I know. Sorry… I'll hop in the shower."

"I dunno. I like you like this."

"Oh yeah? You like my jock sweat?" Greg laughed.

"That sounds like a line from a really bad porno. Just sayin', you look sexy in those running shorts and muscle shirt."

"It's an old tank top, but thanks."

"With you wearin' it, it's a muscle shirt." It fit him snugly, the fabric hugging his pecs to reveal the outline of his chiseled chest. Bryan drank in the sight of his broad shoulders and bulging biceps. He felt a stirring beneath the covers.

"You have a nice body yourself," Greg said. "We should work out together."

"You have the perfect build," Bryan said, and then he picked up his sandwich and began unwrapping it. "Not too bulky, but very toned."

"Thanks. It's kind of an obsession. Maybe I'm vain. I don't know. But I've just always hated the stereotypes. Back in high school, when I first came out, I was paranoid about being labeled. People think all gay guys are girly, into drama club and high fashion. I didn't want to be perceived that way, so I focused on being as manly as possible. It was really shallow of me, I know. And at this point, I don't care about any of that anymore, but I'm kind of addicted to the physical fitness."

"Would you date someone like that? I mean, someone who was fem?"

Greg looked up, over Bryan's head, as if thinking. "Hm, probably. Well, yeah, I know I would. Look at Ian—he's not exactly macho. And I've dated other guys who weren't into sports or physical fitness."

"Like Adam and Trevor. Trevor's not athletic at all."

Greg laughed. "And look what a great couple they are. I think we get too hung up on being 'straight-acting.' It doesn't matter, though, because right now there's only one guy I'm interested in dating, and he's hot as fuck."

"Who could that be, girlfriend?" Bryan gestured with his hand, flopping his wrist in an exaggerated manner. With his other hand he snapped his fingers in the air.

Greg laughed. "Hey, Trevor's rubbing off on you."

Bryan's mouth dropped open in shock. "Oh, that's bad. You better not let Adam hear you say that."

He rolled his eyes, then grinned. "I love Trevor. He's a cutie, but he can get a bit fired up. He's so feisty and campy."

"He's hilarious. You know, he's probably my best friend now. That's so weird, because I used to be so prejudiced against guys like him. My friend Evan's boyfriend Noah is kind of fem, and I used to hate him. It's weird how we can change our opinions of people when we get to know them better. I was such a jerk."

"You've grown, and that's a good thing. I'm guilty of the same thing, which is probably why I ran for president of the student union. Last year, when I was a freshman, I started going to the meetings and became friends with a lot of people who were really different than me. Different than the type of people I thought I wanted as friends. I wanted to be a voice for them."

Bryan thought about it. That was kind of how he viewed Evan and Adam. They were the type of guys who could blend in so easily. Unless they wanted to come out to someone, they could conceal their sexual orientation with little effort. But not all gay people were like that. Some people were automatically perceived as gay; they were noticeably different. It was cool that Greg didn't think this made him any better. He was one of them.

"Don't you think there's a lot of snobbery, though? I mean, most of the time the good-looking, butch guys act like they're so much better than the fems or the nerdy guys or the people who are really shy."

"Yeah." He nodded. "But that's true of all people... unfortunately. And it also cuts both ways. There have been times I've tried to befriend people and they've rejected me, assuming I was some kind of snob or something just because of the way I look."

Bryan recalled his first impression of Greg. "I thought you were a rich spoiled brat."

"I *wish*. Well, I guess I am kind of spoiled. I'm far from rich, though. When Dad died, my college was paid for. And Mom had enough insurance money for us to live comfortably, but most of that's gone now. With her health problems, we really don't have much savings. Thankfully the house is paid off, and I don't have a car payment or anything."

"You could get a roommate," Bryan suggested.

"I've been thinking about that," Greg said, and then he reached out to take hold of Bryan's hand. "But I need to wait. I have to see how Mom does."

"I understand." Bryan nodded. Greg probably thought he was asking for an invitation to move in. "And I didn't mean to make it sound like I wanted to move in with you. I, uh...."

"Oh, I know. But it's a nice thought." Greg leaned in and kissed him once more.

CHAPTER
— 14 —

"DOES IT count when you tell someone you love them while in the throes of passion?"

Traci set down the napkin she was folding and leaned against the bar. "All right, spill! You guys did it finally."

"Is that a question or a statement?"

"Statement. I just want the juicy details!" She stepped around the counter and grabbed Bryan by the shoulders. "And don't spare *any*thing."

Bryan laughed, then shrugged, trying as best he could to seem casual. "Well, after Greg won the tournament, we stopped and got burgers, then went back to his house, where I fucked his brains out."

Her jaw unhinged as she stood there with her hands on her hips. "So *you* fucked *him*?"

"Is that so hard to believe?" Bryan feigned indignation. "Actually, it was very beautiful. We're both versatile, if you must know, and believe me, he had his turn the next morning."

"You guys are so adorable. I can just picture it."

Bryan made a face, realizing he'd probably shared too much. "Please don't." He laughed.

"What? Why is it okay for straight guys to fantasize about two chicks doing the nasty, but if it's a woman fantasizing about two gay guys, she's a pervert or something?"

"It's not that," Bryan said. "It's just that when one of those guys is me...."

"Well, take it as a compliment."

He extended his arms and pulled her in for a hug. "Oh, I know. And yeah, it was wonderful, but you didn't answer my question."

"Hm. Well, I think it's possible to shout something out in the heat of passion that you don't really mean, but in your case, I doubt you'd do that. Would you?"

He stepped back, then turned and took a seat at the bar. "We haven't known each other that long, and last night was our first time together."

"True, but you've been getting to know each other, and you've taken things slowly. I mean, I know a lot of gay guys who meet and jump in the sack ten minutes later. Then they're professing their undying love for each other."

"Until the next hot guy comes along."

"Exactly. Bryan, what did he say when you said you loved him?"

Bryan smiled. "I'm not sure. He was busy moaning at the time."

"Oh my God! Did he even hear you?"

Bryan grew serious. "Yeah, he heard me. He'd already told me he loves me."

Traci grabbed hold of his wrist. "Bryan, this is serious."

"I know... I think I've fallen head over heels."

BRYAN WAS texting Greg for the two hundredth time that day as he walked into Hank's office. He notified the receptionist he was there, then took a seat in the waiting room. It had been three days since Bryan had stayed overnight at Greg's, but they'd seen each other every day since. Jeff had dropped Bryan off, but Greg was picking him up in an hour, when Bryan was done with his appointment. They were going to visit Greg's mom, and Bryan was nervous about the first meeting.

The door opened, and another patient exited. Then Hank stepped out behind her. "Bryan, come on in."

Bryan felt upbeat and for once didn't dread the counseling session with Hank. Usually, he hated it. His negative feelings weren't directed at Hank. Bryan actually liked him, but what he didn't like was the probing. He wasn't comfortable exposing himself, laying bare his emotions. The moments Hank regarded as most significant—breakthroughs, as he called them—were the very incidents that made Bryan the most uncomfortable. He was embarrassed by his weakness, by his vulnerability.

"How goes everything this week?" Hank asked as they took their seats.

"Good," Bryan said.

"Good is not an acceptable answer. I want something more descriptive, something specific."

"Okay. *Very* good."

Hank laughed. "All right. Why is everything *very* good this week?"

"Greg won his tennis match. First place."

"Wow, impressive. But what about you, Bryan?"

"I got my first hundred-dollar tip."

"Bet that felt good."

"It felt awesome. And…." Bryan cracked a wide smile.

Apparently the smile was infectious, because Hank began to grin as well. "And…?"

"And we made love."

Hank nodded, still smiling. "And by the look on your face, I think it's safe to say that also went well."

"It was cool. I, um, enjoyed it." Bryan was determined not to let Hank's intrusive questions bother him. He was in too good of a mood, and in a few minutes, he'd be with Greg again. After their visit with Greg's mom, they just might make love again. They might do it all fucking night long… if they felt like it.

"Bryan, have we talked about safe sex? You did use…."

"Yes!" He squirmed a bit in his chair as he felt the heat in his cheeks.

"I don't mean to embarrass you, but I'd be remiss if I didn't remind you of the importance of practicing safe sex, not only for the sake of your physical health, but for your overall mental health."

"Can we just move on?"

Hank folded his hands together and rested them on his knee. His legs were crossed, the same way he always sat. So prim and proper. In some ways he reminded Bryan of Jeff. "Certainly. Well, I'm not surprised to see you in such high spirits. When we embark on a new relationship, particularly a physically intimate relationship, there is a euphoria."

Bryan hated the way Hank was minimizing the significance of what he and Greg had shared. Hank seemed to always know exactly how to rain on his parade. Bryan scowled. "No, it's not like that."

"Oh? Then tell me. If it's not euphoria, then what is it that's heightened your spirits?"

At the moment, Bryan's spirits were plummeting. "This isn't a *new* relationship, for one thing. I've known Greg for almost a month, and we didn't even do anything together right away, not until we were ready."

Hank's expression was smug, and Bryan felt the urge to smack it right off his face. "Bryan, let's review your history. You previously had a significant other, if I remember."

"What's that got to do with Greg?"

"Probably nothing, but like I cautioned you previously, this might not be the best time—"

"I love him! And Greg loves me, so don't tell me this isn't the right time."

Hank straightened his posture but did not break eye contact. "Bryan, slow down."

"Are you saying I don't know how I feel? Well, you're wrong, because I do. I've never felt this way about anyone. Ever."

"I get that." Hank nodded. "But you're eighteen right now, and this is potentially your first serious relationship."

Bryan sighed in an exaggerated manner. "Not true. I was with Liam for, like, three months."

Hank held up his hand, palm out, as if to calm Bryan. But Bryan wasn't about to be placated. What he was about to do was leave—get up and walk out. And he just might tell Hank what he thought of him and his stupid counseling.

"Bryan, rather than jumping into a relationship right now, perhaps you and Greg could—"

"Take things slow. Yeah, I know. And that's exactly what we're doing. I said I love him, not that I wanted to get married."

"At eighteen, most guys aren't ready to settle into a committed relationship long term. The vast majority of people date for a while, experience life a little bit, before they settle down with one partner."

"That's not true. Look at Jeff and Brett. They met in high school and have been together for something like twenty-five years. And my friend Evan, he only had one boyfriend: Noah. They're really happy together, and so are Trevor and Adam."

"And that's great," Hank said. His tone was calm, soothing almost, which made it all the more annoying. Bryan was ready to argue his case, but Hank didn't want to play hardball. "And that might or might not be the case with you and Greg. If it's not, if Greg ends up not being the type of guy who wants to commit to a monogamous relationship, are you going to be okay with that?"

"We haven't even talked about that yet." Bryan was annoyed. "I'm not saying we're the next Jeff and Brett. I'm not saying we're moving in together and getting married. I just really, really like him."

"And that's fine. That's healthy and reasonable. But what you initially said was that you were in love."

"No, I said I love him. There's a big difference."

Hank nodded slowly. "In Hollywood movies, young couples fall in love and live happily ever after. Real life doesn't always happen that way."

Perhaps the reason Hank's caveats were so disturbing to Bryan was because they were all things he'd considered. Bryan wasn't even old enough to get into a gay bar. He'd just started school, a huge campus with tons of gay guys. Even though Greg seemed perfect for him, would he always feel that way? He was young, and this was the time of his life when he should be having fun, playing the field. If the relationship with Greg developed into something serious, something long term like Jeff and Brett had, would he one day look back and regret it?

"Greg's picking me up in a few minutes, and we're going to visit his mom. She's in a home or something."

"Oh?"

"Yeah. She has really bad depression, or… I don't know exactly…. Some type of illness. And, um, she had a breakdown."

Hank frowned but didn't immediately say anything. "How much of your treatment plan have you shared with Greg, if you don't mind me asking?"

Actually, he did kind of mind. He answered anyway. "He knows everything, and he's very supportive. Greg's in premed, and he plans to become a psychologist."

Hank's mouth dropped open slightly as he raised his eyebrows.

BRYAN FELT like butterflies were flitting around in his stomach. He sat in the passenger seat of Greg's car, holding Greg's hand, and he wasn't sure if the feeling he was experiencing was a result of nervousness about meeting Greg's mom, or a bit of angst over the questions raised in his counseling session. Still, holding Greg's hand was pretty awesome.

Ever since they'd spent the night together, Greg had been at the forefront of Bryan's thoughts. Hardly a moment went by where Bryan wasn't thinking about Greg, smiling to himself, sometimes even whistling or humming. Perhaps this high really was a state of euphoria, an infatuation. What if this meant Hank was right and what if this relationship didn't prove to be long-standing, like Jeff and Brett's venerable relationship?

"Can I ask you something?" Bryan finally mustered the courage to bring up his concerns to Greg.

"Anything, babe."

"I know it's none of my business, and it really doesn't matter to me, but…."

Greg glanced over to him. "Should I maybe pull over and park somewhere for this conversation?" He chuckled, and Bryan responded by shaking his head.

"No, it's really nothing. I just wondered about how many guys you'd been with."

"Okay. I'm pulling over."

"I feel stupid now."

Greg laughed. "No, don't be silly." He turned into a shopping plaza and whipped into an empty parking space. Once the vehicle was in park, he shifted in his seat to face Bryan directly, still holding on to his hand. "Are you asking how many guys I've slept with? Or relationships?"

"I, um, I just wondered if you'd had a boyfriend before? Long term, I mean."

Greg nodded. "Sure. I dated this one guy in high school for over a year. His name was Marcus."

"And what happened?"

"I don't know exactly. What can I say? It was a high-school romance, replete with all manner of drama. I mean, I really liked him… a lot. But it never got to a point where I was starting to think about a future with him. I guess we kind of grew apart. He started seeing other people, then I did the same, and we kind of mutually agreed it was over."

Bryan furrowed his brow, thinking how to proceed, whether or not he should ask his next question. "And now… how do you feel?"

"About you?"

Bryan nodded.

"Bryan… *babe*, there's no comparison of you to Marcus. That was a high school thing. Puppy love."

"But look at Adam and Trevor. They met in high school, and so did Galen and Todd. Even Jeff and Brett started dating when they were in school."

Greg shrugged. "I think there are some couples who meet and experience love at first sight. They're lucky, but I don't think you should make comparisons of yourself—or us—to them. To be honest, I really don't think that's typical. Most people don't stay with their high school sweetheart for life."

"I guess maybe I'm overthinking it."

"You totally are. And you know what? I don't want to spend my time worrying about that sort of thing. I know how I feel about you right now, and I want to enjoy it rather than worrying about putting a label on it."

Bryan bit his lower lip, then squeezed Greg's hand. He leaned in and kissed him softly on the lips. "You're right. I don't wanna worry about it either."

"I think we'll both know when and if it's time to take our relationship to the next step."

"And what will that be?"

"Anyone ever tell you how cute you are when you fret about things?"

Bryan rolled his eyes, laughing. "You're avoiding my question."

"All right, just let say this." He raised his hand, palm outward. "Scout's honor, you're the first guy I've ever said 'I love you' to."

Bryan hadn't realized he'd been holding his breath, but when he exhaled, it felt like a weight had been lifted from his chest. He opened his mouth to speak, but suddenly choked up. "Me too," he managed to eke out.

"And I don't want to see other guys; I want us to be exclusive."

"Me too!"

"And wherever that leads us, we'll follow. I have faith in you, Bryan. I have faith in *us*."

"You're totally right. These past three days have been the most awesome time of my life. I've been floating on a cloud, and I can't stop thinking about you. But then today, I just kind of freaked. I was worried you might not feel the same way about me, that you might think it's silly of me to get so serious about you this fast."

"I don't think it's silly, and I feel the same way. Do you think I'd be texting you a zillion times a day? Do you think I'd call you and hook up with you every day if I wasn't absolutely crazy about you?"

"No." Bryan shook his head.

Greg leaned in, taking hold of Bryan's face with both hands, framing it with his palms, and kissed him tenderly on the lips. As Bryan responded, the kiss grew in intensity and morphed into a passionate make-out session. That wasn't the only thing that grew. Soon they were fogging up the windows. Greg pulled back suddenly and turned in his seat. He glanced in his rearview mirror and shifted the gear column into reverse. He peeled out of the parking space, then sped around to the back of the shopping complex. Bryan was still gasping for breath when Greg parked the car in a secluded area behind one of the dumpsters.

"What are we doing?" Bryan asked.

Greg leaned over and unfastened the clasp of Bryan's seat belt, then he reached for Bryan's groin. Bryan's jaw unhinged as Greg unzipped his pants and peeled back Bryan's fly. Three seconds later, he moaned as Greg's mouth engulfed his raging hard-on.

IT DIDN'T look like a medical facility. It was a home, just an ordinary ranch-style house in a typical suburban neighborhood. Bryan stood behind Greg, waiting for someone to answer the doorbell.

"It's not exactly what I expected," Bryan admitted.

"Yeah, it's a fairly laid-back environment. Feels more like a home than a hospital. Well, that's what it is, actually. It's a group home."

"Greg!" The door had flung open and before them stood a middle-aged Latina woman, beaming from ear to ear. She stepped out and extended her arms, then engulfed Greg in a fierce bear hug.

"Maria, I was hoping you'd be working."

"Oh yes, of course. I always work Thursdays. Your mama is going to be so happy to see you. And who is this gorgeous young man you have with you?" Bryan grinned as he soaked in the praise. There was such warmth in her demeanor, and her eyes sparkled with sincerity.

"This is Bryan, my boyfriend."

Boyfriend! Bryan's stomach somersaulted.

"Oh, how wonderful to meet you, Bryan."

He extended his hand, but she ignored it, stepped into his personal space, and pulled him into a hug. Bryan responded by hugging back, and laughed in spite of himself.

"Your mama is out back, enjoying the sun on the terrace," Maria said as she ushered them inside. "I'll walk you out there."

Bryan looked around the spacious living room. A couple of women sat in the chairs watching television, which played at low volume. They were engrossed in some reality show, but they both looked up and smiled.

"Hi, Gloria. Hi, Elaine," Greg said, smiling.

They both waved and said hello, obviously charmed by Greg's friendliness. He seemed to have that effect on most people.

Maria led the way through the kitchen and dining room and then over to a sliding glass door at the back of the building. She pulled it open, and Bryan followed Greg across the threshold out onto a veranda.

Bryan recognized Greg's mother immediately. She had Greg's eyes and the same color hair. But the lines on her face told a tale of their own. She looked tired, but her face lit up with a radiant smile when she spotted her son. She was holding a cigarette, but she quickly disposed of it in an ashtray on the table, then pushed herself up into a standing position as Greg walked over and hugged her.

"Mom, I thought you quit...."

"Oh... I'm trying." She reached up and swiped a loose strand of hair from her forehead, then cocked her head to the right. "It was my first one today."

Bryan looked down at the overflowing ashtray and wondered if it might not be a fib.

"Mom, I want you to meet someone," Greg said. "This is my friend Bryan."

"Hi." Bryan stepped closer, smiling.

"Bryan's really special to me."

"Oh, how wonderful to meet you." She held out her hand, and Bryan took hold of it, patting it with his opposite hand.

"It's my pleasure, Mrs. Lewis."

"Allison," she corrected.

"Allison."

"Would you two like something to drink?" Maria asked. "An iced tea, maybe?"

"Oh God, Maria, that sounds wonderful," Greg said.

She looked at Bryan expectantly.

"Sure, that would be nice. Thank you."

As Maria headed back to the kitchen, the three of them took their seats at the patio table.

There was no awkward moment of silence because Greg immediately began talking, asking his mom about her week, pressing her for details about what she'd done, how she was feeling. She reached down beside her chair into a canvas bag and retrieved a scarf she was knitting, showing it to the two of them.

"I'm making these for Doug's boys," she said.

"Doug's my dad's brother, my uncle," Greg explained. "They live in Wisconsin."

That made sense. There wouldn't be much use for winter scarves around here. It was mid-October and the temperature was nearly ninety degrees.

The thing that struck Bryan was the way Greg focused on his mom and her well-being. He would have thought the first thing Greg would tell her was that he'd won his tournament, but when it did finally come up in conversation, Greg was flippant about it, dismissing it as if it were no big deal.

Allison was charming, like her son, and Bryan struggled a bit to wrap his mind around the reality that she was sick. She seemed perfectly normal, in a great mood, just like any other mom.

When Maria returned with their beverages, she sat down with them and visited awhile. The atmosphere was so relaxed it seemed like they were at a normal house, having tea on the lanai and chatting, rather than visiting a sick relative in a care facility. Bryan almost forgot where they were and why they were there.

Both ladies appeared genuinely interested in Bryan, asking him about college and where he was from. The four of them talked about the country club and experiences Greg and Bryan had at work. They talked about Bryan and Greg's college experience, and Greg told his mom about the upcoming fund-raiser. Maria promised to stop by with her car for the car wash.

After a few minutes, Maria tried to excuse herself, insisting that she actually go do some work. Allison pshawed her, laughing and encouraging her to stay and visit. She stayed another fifteen minutes until she finally pushed herself up from her chair and announced she had to go begin preparing dinner.

"You two are welcome to stay," Allison said.

"Oh, I'm not sure," Greg said. "I don't think you're allowed to invite your guests to stay for dinner." He laughed. "Besides, Bryan and I kind of have plans."

We do?

"We really should get going, but I'm gonna try to come back this weekend. Maybe we can go shopping or something. I'll take *you* out for dinner."

"That would be nice, but I know how busy you are."

"I'm really not, not anymore. Now that I've got the tournament behind me, I've got all kinds of free time."

She shook her head. "And you have this adorable young man here." She motioned toward Bryan. "You should be spending time together."

"Bryan can come with us, then, if he wants."

They both turned to him, smiling. "I'd love to," he said, and he meant it.

Finally they stood and exchanged hugs. When Bryan embraced Allison, he noted how frail she was. She was skinny, a rack of bones, and smelled of soap and stale tobacco. She kissed him on the cheek. Allison then grabbed hold of her son and moaned as she pulled him into herself, squeezing him tightly.

"I love you."

"I love you so much, Mom. If you need anything, call me any time. Day or night."

"Okay." Tears welled in her eyes, and Bryan felt a bit misty-eyed himself.

When they climbed back into the car, Bryan was still smiling, amazed by the experience. The group home was nothing like what he'd expected. He could see why Allison would be comfortable there. He took Greg's hand in his own after they backed out of the driveway, then turned to look up into his face.

Rivulets of tears streamed down Greg's cheeks.

CHAPTER
— 15 —

ADMITTEDLY, BRYAN wasn't all that much of a morning person. In general, he hated his fucking alarm clock, and on more than one occasion had considered smashing it to smithereens. Usually he felt like that when he had to be up early for class or work and hadn't gotten a full night's sleep. He'd been working more hours, his confidence level growing as he mastered the skills of hospitality and customer service. Classes were going well, and even his counseling sessions were tolerable. Most importantly, though, his relationship with Greg was idyllic, almost too good to be true.

The more time he and Greg spent together, the deeper his feelings grew. Most evenings they saw each other, when they weren't working, that was. They'd begun going to the youth group events, a few college parties, and at least two or three nights per week, Bryan stayed over at Greg's house.

Today they were taking some time off, just for themselves, away from work and school, and going with Adam and Trevor to Busch Gardens for a fun-filled day of sun, water, and carnival rides. He'd never been there, but Trevor had described it as being a zoo/amusement park combo. It wasn't exactly Gay Days at Disney World, but the foursome would have their own gay celebration.

So when the alarm went off that morning, Bryan didn't engage in his typical ritual of slamming the snooze button three or four times. Instead, his feet hit the floor within seconds of the alarm sounding. He yawned and flipped off the buzzer, then stumbled across the room, stopping to scoop up a T-shirt he'd thrown on the floor. He slipped it over his head, then ambled out into the hallway and into the bathroom.

After taking care of business and hopping in the shower, Bryan headed back to his bedroom to get dressed and preen in front of the mirror. He silently prayed for a good hair day.

One thing Bryan did every day after getting up was take his medication, accompanied by the mandatory eight ounces of water. He usually grabbed a bottled water from the fridge, took his pill, and chugged the water on his way out the door to school, work, or wherever he was going. Once he felt comfortable that he was presentable enough to be seen by another human being, he dashed down the hall and descended the staircase, heading for the kitchen. Jeff was already up, by the stove flipping pancakes, when Bryan breezed past him and grabbed his bottled water from the refrigerator.

"Morning," Jeff said cheerfully. "You're bright-eyed and bushy tailed today."

Bryan laughed and tried not to roll his eyes. Where did Jeff come up with some of the quirky things he said? "Yeah, playing hooky for the whole weekend." He grinned as he rested his hand on Jeff's shoulder. "Mm, those smell good. Blueberry?"

"These are blueberry, and I'm also making chocolate chip."

"Oh. My. God. You're killing me! Chocolate chip are my favorite."

"Good. Breakfast will be served in about ten minutes, so get a move on."

Bryan raised both hands in the air, one of them containing the water bottle. "Hey, I'm totally ready this morning."

"If only you were like this every morning. You're worse than Adam."

Bryan took Jeff's criticism as a compliment. It made him feel like one of the boys, a member of the family. "You boys are going to Busch Gardens for the weekend. Brett's going golfing, and I've got the whole place to myself. Heaven!" He set down his spatula and rubbed his hands together.

"Let me guess. You're gonna binge-watch reality TV. The Kardashians?" Jeff picked the spatula back up and made to swat at his behind, but Bryan quickly sidestepped him, laughing. "Just kidding."

"I'm gonna curl up with a good, steamy, trashy, sexy novel and a really strong vodka tonic. Veg all day until I'm utterly shitfaced."

"Yeah, right." Bryan had never seen Jeff so much as tipsy. "I'd like to see that."

Jeff laughed. "No, but it's been a week from Hell, and I *am* gonna just kick back and relax. Hey, you all set on your meds? You should be due for a refill."

"Uh, yeah, I think so. I'll let ya know. I'm going to take 'em now, then I'll be right back down for breakfast." He headed back upstairs, passing Trevor in the hall.

"Morning, sunshine!" Trevor said.

Bryan shook his head. "Is this whole family a bunch of weirdos?"

"Yes!" Adam stuck his head out of the bathroom, toothbrush hanging out of his mouth. He removed it, holding it in his fist. "Especially Trevor and Dad. They're fucking morning people."

Bryan laughed and slipped back into his bedroom. He picked up the pill bottle and popped open the cap. When he looked inside, he realized it was empty. How had he not noticed he was running low? Shit.

He sat down at his desk and pulled open the top drawer. He'd stashed another bottle in there, but was pretty sure it, too, was empty. He checked it, just to be sure. Also empty.

Oh well, skipping two days of meds wasn't gonna hurt anything. He'd get the prescriptions refilled when he got back home Monday. He wondered exactly how much they helped at this point. He was thinking of telling Hank he wanted to try going off them.

While he was sitting there, he fired up his laptop and logged into his bank account. He'd opened both a checking and savings account after he started working at the restaurant, and he was excited to see how quickly the accounts were growing. Although he handed over his payroll checks to Jeff, he saved the majority of his tip money. He already had amassed over a grand. When the screen came up, he was pleased to see he now had $1342. That's right, he'd made a deposit earlier in the week.

He pulled out his phone and texted Greg, telling him to hurry up and get over here. Breakfast was about ready. Greg replied that he was on his way but not to wait for him because he didn't know if he'd make it in time to eat. Bryan knew Jeff would save him a plate.

When Bryan got back downstairs, the table was set and Brett and the boys were already seated. Bryan took his place beside Trevor and informed them Greg was running a little late and said to eat without him.

"I'll save some batter and make him some hot flapjacks when he gets here," Jeff said from the kitchen. "Did you check your pills?"

"Uh, yeah. I'm all set for now. I got enough till next week."

"Okay. I'll call in your refill and pick it up."

"Um, wait. I was thinking…."

"Don't do that," Adam said. "Remember what happened the last time you tried thinking."

"Very funny," Bryan said sarcastically. "Anyway, I can afford to get my prescription. I've been making some awesome tips."

Brett spoke up. "We'll get it." It was more like a command than an offer. "Jeff or I can pick up the prescription. In fact, call it in and I'll swing by the pharmacy this afternoon."

"Sir," Bryan said, attempting to convey his utmost respect. "I appreciate it, but it'd mean a lot to me if you could let me buy the pills myself this time. I don't want to…."

Jeff and Brett exchanged a look, and Bryan glanced over to Trevor, who was taking a sip of his orange juice. He raised his eyebrows but didn't say anything.

"Let us cover it this time, Bryan," Brett said. "It's probably the last time we'll have to worry about it. Your insurance kicks in on January 1."

Bryan knew it was pointless to argue. He wanted to tell them to just never mind, that he was going to talk to talk to Hank about discontinuing the meds. But he knew this wasn't the right time to discuss it. "Okay. I really appreciate it."

BRYAN HAD to laugh. He'd talked to Evan on the phone the night before and learned they'd already gotten snow in Michigan. Had he not moved to Florida, he'd be bundled up right now, hoping not to freeze his nuts off in twenty-degree weather. Instead, here he was in a tank top and bathing suit, soaring down the river rapids with his hot sexy boyfriend and his two best buds.

In addition to the water rides, the park had a slew of roller coasters, which happened to be Bryan's favorite. In Michigan they didn't have many choices when it came to amusement parks. The weather in that part of the country simply wasn't conducive to a year-round theme park. The short summer season wasn't long enough for an attraction like that to be lucrative. His hometown of Boyne City offered an indoor water park, and there was a midsized park in Muskegon, about three hours south of where he'd lived. During the summer, he'd vacationed in Sandusky, Ohio to visit Cedar Point, but that was about six hours away by car.

While at Busch Gardens, Bryan used his phone to take lots of pictures, more than half of which were of Greg, and they snapped a selfie while on the Montu, the freakiest of all the rides. It was like being strapped into a large swing-set seat and then whipped through a series of terrifying loops at something like a thousand miles per hour.

When they got off the ride, Bryan was cracking up. "I thought you were gonna shit yourself," he teased Greg.

"I think Trevor *did* shit himself," Adam said. The two of them were right behind Greg and Bryan. "Smells like it."

Trevor slugged him, then gave him a shove. "Shut up. I wasn't even scared."

Adam grabbed hold of him and planted a sloppy kiss on the cheek. "It's okay, baby. I'll protect you."

"Get away from me, you Neanderthal."

"Aw, you still love me."

In spite of himself, Trevor broke into a smile. "It *was* pretty scary."

They headed over to a concession stand. Bryan was dying of thirst. "It costs, like, five bucks for a bottled water here."

"Crazy," Greg said. "I want a hot dog or something."

The four of them decided food sounded good, and they got in line. When they got up to the window, Greg placed an order for Bryan and him and pulled out his wallet.

"I can get it," Bryan said.

"Nah. My treat this time. You paid for the admission tickets." Bryan liked that about Greg, that he let Bryan treat him but also reciprocated.

He nodded his assent, then waited as Greg placed the order. The young guy who waited on them had blond hair and a cute face. His perfect, pearly white teeth made for a killer smile. He was extremely friendly, and had a thick southern accent.

"Hey, did you go to Hillsborough?" Greg asked.

"Yeah, I sure did. I thought you looked familiar. I'm James."

"Damn! Small world. You in school around here now?"

"UT," James said.

"No kidding. That's where we go. I'm president of the LGBT student union."

"Awesome. I've been meaning to go to a meeting or something."

"You should. We're meeting again next week, and we're doing some events down at the Pride Center. Looking for volunteers. Hot guys—like you—to help with our car wash."

"Sure, man. You got a card or something?"

Greg pulled out a business card from his wallet. "Gimme your number, if you don't mind." He already had his phone in hand, and he typed in James's number. As they were leaving, James winked at him.

"Y'all be sure to call me."

"I will," Greg promised.

When they got over to a table and sat down, Bryan began to feel a bit insecure about the whole exchange. He'd been standing right beside Greg, and he hadn't even bothered introducing Bryan to his friend. Of course, they'd been in line, and people had been waiting behind them.

Still, it seemed odd the way James and Greg had flirted so openly, especially with Bryan standing right there.

"You okay?" Greg asked. He offered Bryan a napkin.

"Uh, sure. I guess."

Greg smiled, apparently unsure how to interpret Bryan's remark. "Does this have anything to do with James?"

"No," Bryan said, a little too quickly. He paused, opening his mouth to speak again, but then thought better of it.

"Yes, it does. You're jealous."

Bryan shook his head. "No, I'm not. Don't be silly. You're right, we do need volunteers. And he's cute. He'll be perfect for the car wash."

"Right, so what's the problem?"

"Who said there was a problem?"

Trevor and Adam were still up at the concession window, and Bryan wished they'd hurry up. He just wanted to forget the incident and move on.

"Just the way you were acting. It seemed like you were pissed or something."

Bryan sighed. "I wasn't pissed, but I thought it was weird you didn't even bother to introduce me. I mean, it seems like you gave him the impression that you're single. You even got his number...."

"I got his number so I could call him to remind him to come to the meeting, and to contact him about the car wash." There was a defensive tone to Greg's voice. He'd never talked to Bryan like that before. Well, at least not since they'd started seeing each other.

Bryan nodded. "You're right. I'm sorry. Guess I was a little jealous."

"I probably should have introduced you, babe." Greg slid his arm beneath the table and rested a hand on Bryan's thigh. "It's just we were in line. I think it was kind of obvious to him that we were together, though."

"I know," Bryan said. "I overreacted."

Greg leaned in and offered a conciliatory kiss. "You're kinda cute when you get jealous."

"Shut up," Bryan said, laughing.

WHEN THE foursome had originally planned their excursion to Busch Gardens, they talked about renting motel rooms and having a minivacation not far from home. Bryan, ever the pragmatist, thought the idea was appealing but not practical. "Why waste all that money when we live here? We should just all go back to Greg's house and have a sleepover."

So that was what they did. Adam, now old enough to legally purchase alcohol, picked up a case of Coronas from the liquor store, along with a pint of vodka for Trevor, who wasn't much of a drinker and had zero tolerance for beer. Greg and Bryan showered together when they got home, while Adam and Trevor settled down in front of the TV.

They then spent thirty minutes arguing over what to watch on Netflix. Trevor wanted to see a romantic comedy or drama while Adam and Greg voted for action-adventure. They compromised by selecting an action movie that contained a romance and was laced with sardonic humor.

By the time the movie was over, the four of them were starting to feel the effects of the alcohol. Bryan—who hadn't drank anything, not even at the few frat parties he'd attended since he left Michigan—noticed how buzzed he was when he went to stand up.

"Holy fuck," he said, staggering a bit. He laughed and leaned against the wall to steady himself. He was trying to make his way upstairs to the restroom.

"Oh my God," Trevor teased, "you're more of a lightweight than me."

It was true. Up in Michigan, when Bryan had been with Liam, he drank quite a bit. They were underage, but it had never been hard to find a buyer. After his meltdown, when he'd tried to kill himself, Bryan had avoided alcohol altogether. It seemed to affect him in the exact opposite manner than he desired, amplifying his depression to the point of making him weepy. That wasn't his idea of a good time.

"You okay, babe?" Greg asked.

"Yeah." He laughed it off and stumbled over to the staircase, where he grabbed hold of the railing. Before he could take another step, Greg was at his side, wrapping his arm around Bryan's waist.

Bryan looked at him, staring directly into his eyes, and was instantly overwhelmed with a sweeping surge of emotion. "I love you so much," he gushed. "You're... you're, like, my hero. My knight in shining armor."

The other three guys, including Greg, laughed. "Aw, you know I am."

"I don't know why—" The words caught in his throat. "I don't know why you even care, why you love someone like me."

The smile on Greg's face faded. He pulled Bryan into his body and held him. "Shh. Don't say things like that. You know I don't like that."

"But it's true! You know, I look at myself in the mirror, and sometimes I wonder... is this even me? And how can someone so perfect, so gorgeous and smart and totally awesome like *you*... how can you love me?"

"Come on, I'll help you. Grab hold of the railing."

Bryan wasn't about to cooperate. Instead of reaching for the banister, he wrapped both arms around Greg and pulled him in for a kiss—a passionate, though sloppy, wet kiss. His emotions were beginning to short-circuit, so jumbled Bryan didn't really know what he was feeling. Sad one second, then overjoyed. "I'm so lucky!"

"I think you've had enough to drink for tonight, Bry. How many beers did you have?"

"No! No, we're just getting started. I need another beer." He pulled away from Greg and charged toward the kitchen, completely forgetting he had to use the bathroom. "Where's that fuckin' Corona?"

"Bryan!" Trevor came up beside him and put his hand on Bryan's shoulder. "We don't wanna drink anymore tonight. Why don't we save the rest of these?"

"What are you talking about? Of course we wanna drink." He spun around to look down into Trevor's face. So serious, and so cute with his spikey, jet-black hair and oversized glasses. "You are such a doll, do you know that? You… you and Adam. You're like my best friends in the whole world!" He extended both arms and pulled Trevor into a fierce hug. "I love you guys so much!"

Trevor was smiling as he pushed himself back, separating himself from Bryan's powerful embrace. Greg was now behind Bryan, draping his arm around Bryan's shoulder. "We love you too," Trevor said, "but don't you have to go to the bathroom?"

Bryan straightened his posture, then craned his neck to look over at Greg. "Right. Yeah, I'm sorry. I gotta go pee. I gotta go real bad."

"Come on," Greg said, his tone calm and steady. "Let me help you."

"You're gonna help me pee?" Bryan laughed. He laughed hard and loud, doubling over and hugging himself. "You're gonna help me take a fucking piss!" It struck him as so funny, the most hilarious thing he'd ever heard. "I didn't know you were into water sports!"

His words might not have been as amusing to his friends, but the three of them were all laughing right along with him. Laughter was that way, he supposed. Infectious.

Greg did finally help him upstairs and stood behind him as he relieved himself. He then led Bryan back downstairs to the sofa, where they curled up together, Bryan resting his head in the crook of Greg's shoulder. He wrapped his arm around Greg's torso and held him, listening to his heartbeat as Adam started the next movie. That was the last thing Bryan remembered until he woke up the following morning in Greg's queen-size bed.

"Oh my God," he moaned. "My head!"

CHAPTER
— 16 —

BRYAN RODE home with Adam and Trevor Sunday afternoon. Embarrassed by what he remembered of his behavior the night before, he apologized. They laughed it off, assuring him it was no big deal. Even Greg didn't seem bothered. That morning, when they woke up, they'd made passionate love, and Greg even admitted to Bryan how flattered he was that Bryan had called him a hero, his knight in shining armor.

Overall, Saturday had been awesome—spending the day at Busch Gardens, soaking in the sun and going on all the cool rides. Now, fully energized and refueled, it was time to refocus. His coursework was mounting at college, and he had a busy work schedule. For the next couple weeks he had to concentrate, put his nose to the grindstone.

When he got home and walked into his room, the first thing Bryan noticed was the white pharmacy bag on his desk. Brett, true to his word, had filled the prescription. Now on day two of skipping his medication, he knew he should take a pill. He flopped down on the bed, though. He'd do it later. He didn't feel like going downstairs for a bottle of water.

As he closed his eyes, he recalled being with Greg, how they'd made love a few hours previously. The experience was perhaps the most passionate and intense yet. Greg had been in the mood to top him, and Bryan loved that. He honestly liked it even more than when he assumed the active position. Having Greg inside him, feeling his strength and power, succumbing to Greg's will—damn! His cock was hard now, just thinking about it.

Greg wasn't a selfish lover, though. Not in the least. He was attentive and thoughtful, ever aware of Bryan's satisfaction and pleasure. He did fuck Bryan hard when he sensed Bryan wanted or needed it, yet he never pressured Bryan. And he also was receptive of Bryan's advances. When Bryan wanted to top, Greg was eager and accommodating.

None of this was surprising, not when Bryan thought about it. It made sense that Greg would be such a great lover. Wasn't he all but perfect in every aspect of his life? A straight-A student, president of the student union, a leader at work, champion tennis player—the list went on and on. As much as Bryan admired, even idolized Greg, he did at times feel inadequate. Yeah, he'd gotten drunk last night and said some stupid things, but some of them were grounded in truth. He did wonder what it was about himself that Greg found so attractive.

Bryan knew these thoughts to be distortions. He'd learned that from Hank, and even Jeff had told him as much. Bryan tended to magnify things. He often generalized and made assumptions that weren't necessarily true. All this, according to Hank, was part of his illness. The distorted thought process was a result of the depression, and it was a daily challenge to identify and root out those distortions.

For example, when he began to think that Greg was perfect, so much better than himself, the logical part of his brain knew this wasn't true. Greg was a normal person—flawed like the rest of the human race. He had wonderful qualities that Bryan loved, but Bryan himself was a good person too. He also had a lot going for him, a lot to be proud of. Bryan had done exceedingly well in his new job. He was doing fine in school. He was beginning to prove to himself he could be responsible, hold down a job while going to school, and save up some money. He had no reason to doubt himself all the time.

There were moments when he got disgusted. Nobody liked a person who wallowed in self-pity, and he didn't want to be that way. Good Lord, consider Trevor, or even his friend Todd. They'd both grown up in abject poverty, raised in a run-down, dilapidated trailer park. Trevor had shown him one day, and Bryan couldn't believe it. Now here they were, doing well. He didn't hear them whining and complaining about how miserable their lives were. Bryan had no right to feel sorry for himself.

He had a family now, a family more awesome than any he could have imagined. It was time to just get over it.

Yeah, his parents were jerks. But a lot of people had asshole parents. This was real life, not *Leave It to Beaver*. Bryan knew it was time for him to buck up, pull himself up by the bootstraps, and stop bellyaching. He had a great boyfriend, a good job, a beautiful family, and an overall good life. Most importantly, he had a promising future.

He didn't need the medication anymore. It was a crutch. He really didn't even need the counseling, either. He'd finish out his remaining sessions with Hank, but only because he'd promised to do so. He owed it to Jeff to keep his word, but come January 1, he wasn't going back.

He slid off the bed and picked up the prescription bag, then opened the desk drawer and tossed the pills inside. No more drugs. Period.

SO MANY people volunteered for the car wash, they were going to have to split the guys into two groups. That was fine by Bryan, simply because it meant he wouldn't have to deal with Ian and Ross. They'd have their own group, and Bryan had every intention of kicking their asses. He was sure that his group could outperform them in terms of raising the most money.

In Bryan's group were Greg, Adam, Trevor, Galen, Todd, Danny, and the new guy, James, whom they'd met at Busch Gardens. Perhaps it was a bit conceited of Bryan to admit, but his group was fucking hot. Half of them were jocks with nice, perfectly toned athletic bodies. Well, Danny was skinny, but he was still a good-looking guy. It was still kind of hard for Bryan to wrap his head around the fact he was trans. And then there was Trevor, the resident geek, and Todd, the brainiac.

Bryan hadn't volunteered to be team captain; it just sort of fell on his shoulders. Greg had told him he thought it would be cool if he led the team, and Bryan had agreed, eager to flex his competitive muscles.

He wanted nothing more than to crush Ian, especially after finding out the cruel things he'd said about Allison, Greg's mom.

And the past few days at work, Bryan had gotten stuck working with Ian, who was constantly running his mouth. Sarcasm and snark spewed from his mouth every time it was open. The night before the car wash, at work, Ian had insinuated that Greg was cheating on Bryan. Greg happened to have the night off, and Ian asked what guy Greg was out fucking while Bryan was at work. Bryan had wanted to deck him, but Traci intervened, pulling Bryan aside and talking him down.

"I swear to God, I'm gonna kick his ass," Bryan threatened.

"Fine, but not here. Do it tomorrow at the car wash… figuratively speaking."

She had a good point. Why should Bryan let that little shit get under his skin like that? The last thing Bryan wanted was to jeopardize his job. Instead he'd focus on leading his team to victory. They'd outshine Ian and his snobby friends by raising the most money, and they'd have a blast in the process.

After work, Greg came over to help make signs. Adam had class, so he couldn't attend, but Trevor was there. Todd also came, without Galen. The four of them used the spacious dining room table to design their poster-board signs. About halfway through, Jeff came home and walked into the middle of their chaos.

"Uh, I'm sorry," Bryan said. "We didn't mean to take over your house."

Jeff scowled, standing there with his arms crossed over his chest. "You could have let me know in advance," he said.

"I know, sir. My bad…. We'll get this cleaned up—"

"So that I could've been here in time to help!" Jeff stepped over to the table, examining the signs. "You have any more poster boards?"

"Sure!"

Jeff ended up ordering them deep-dish pizzas, and the event turned into a party. Jeff promised to make some calls, encouraging his friends and colleagues to be sure to stop by for the event and get their cars washed. Tips, he said, were more than welcome; they'd all be donated to the charity.

"You know what I think would be cool?" Bryan said to the group. "I'd really like it if a portion of the money we raise would go to helping homeless gay teens."

"I don't see why you can't request the Pride Center designate a portion of the money to a specific area of their budget," Jeff said. "I know they have an outreach that works with LGBT kids."

"I mean, I was sort of in that same situation myself. If not for my friend Evan and his mom... and of course, you and Brett... I'd probably be homeless right now."

Jeff stepped over to him and placed his hand on the side of Bryan's face, then kissed him on the forehead.

Bryan, who was sitting at the table, looked up and smiled. "Have I told you how much I love you?"

"You just did," Jeff whispered, his eyes misty with tears.

"I'M NOT taking my shirt off," Todd said.

"It's cool." Bryan rested his hand on Todd's shoulder, squeezing it. "You're cute with or without a shirt." Todd's face reddened, brighter than his strawberry blond hair.

The group of guys had gathered on the lawn in front of Pride Center, right in front of the circular driveway. They had hoses connected to the main building, and a few feet from him, on the other side of the drive, Ian's group had staged their setup.

"Adam and Greg, can you go out by the road with signs? Get the cars to pull into our side of the driveway, using whatever means necessary." They all laughed. "We'll take turns with the signs. Oh, and peel off those shirts!"

Bryan glanced over to the competition, a little worried. Ian had assembled quite the cast of hot bodies. Not only did he have Ross by his side, but a few of the other guys looked an awful lot like porn stars Bryan had seen on the Internet. *Coincidence, I'm sure.*

His own team was pretty damn hot, though, and with Greg and Galen out front, wearing only their skimpy nylon running shorts, they ought to be able to reel in some customers. As they got underway and the first car pulled in, Bryan remembered something important. He picked up the bullhorn on the ground beside him and ran out to the road. "Here," he said, handing it to Greg. "Use this to call out to the cars. And don't be afraid to show some leg."

Greg grinned and shook his head. "How can I *not* show some leg, wearing these?" He held his arms out.

"Uh, good point. I'm gonna start the music. Dance around or something."

By the time he got back to the staging area, the first car was already soaped up. The driver was standing outside beside the vehicle, and Bryan immediately recognized him. "Gerald!" It was his elderly customer from the restaurant, the one who'd given him the hundred-dollar tip. Bryan rushed up to him and offered a hug.

Gerald ran his hands across the smooth skin of Bryan's bare back as he squeezed him. "Oh my, are you trying to give this old man a heart attack?"

"Where's your friend?" Bryan asked.

"Lionel will be along shortly. He's bringing the other vehicle."

"Oh, that's great. So what do ya think?"

Gerald looked around, taking in the young, shirtless guys who were rinsing his car. He placed a hand over his heart. "I think I've already died and gone to heaven."

Bryan laughed. "Did you stay for the tournament that day?"

"Oh, we certainly did. Congratulations to your young man. He was every bit the superstar you said he'd be."

"Excuse me just a second. I've got to get the music going."

Bryan walked over to the boom box they'd brought with them and pressed the play button. The rap music was just the ticket, and soon the guys were moving in rhythm to the beat, leaning across the car as they scrubbed it with their sponges. Bryan looked at Gerald and noticed him staring at Galen's behind. Galen was bent over, and the fabric of his shorts pulled tightly across his sexy bottom.

"Twerk it!" Bryan shouted.

And Galen did exactly that! Holy shit, did he ever.

"Day-um!" Danny shouted. "That boy was born to twerk."

Soon, some of the passersby who were coming and going to and from the building stopped to watch, and a crowd started gathering. James was the next one to give it a try, and as he placed his palms on the hood of the car and thrust his bottom outward, Bryan burst into laughter. "Work it, boy!"

Soon Danny and Trevor joined in, then the guys out by the road. Bryan even decided to try mimicking their butt-jiggling. Catcalls and cheers erupted as onlookers began applauding. Even self-conscious Todd gave it a try, just briefly.

For the next two hours they twerked their butts off, and the cars continued to line up. When Jeff and Brett arrived with their vehicles, Brett had them all in hysterics. He was the first middle-aged guy Bryan had ever seen twerking, and Bryan about went into convulsions, he was laughing so hard.

Bryan was in charge of handling the cash box, and he was so busy with his customers, he didn't even look over at the other group. He completely forgot about his competition until a few minutes before the end of the event. When he did glance over, his heart sank. The other group looked just as busy as his.

Oh well, he thought. It was for a great cause. He was happy they'd raised so much money and the event was successful. It really didn't matter who won or lost.

Around three o'clock that afternoon, they started to wrap everything up, and Bryan picked up his cash box and headed for the Pride Center office. Greg rushed over to him and planted a passionate kiss on his lips. "You were fantastic today," Greg said. "I'm so proud of you!"

"Thanks." Bryan beamed. "We're a team, though. We all worked hard. I wanna get this money inside. I can't wait to find out how much we made."

"Let me grab my shirt and I'll come with you," he said.

"Okay, I'll wait here by the door."

As Greg dashed across the lawn, Bryan noticed Ross heading toward the building. He was carrying a zippered bank bag, apparently what their team had used for storing their donations. Ross was still shirtless, and as he strutted across the parking lot, Bryan couldn't help but notice his awesome physique.

He looked away, choosing to stare at his own boyfriend instead. Greg had made it over to the lawn area where he'd tossed his T-shirt. He stooped to pick it up, and as he did so, James stepped over to him. Bryan continued to watch them, noticing as James reached out and ran his palm across Greg's lower back while Greg was still bent over. As Greg stood upright, James slipped his hand lower, and Bryan saw him gently squeeze Greg's asscheek. Bryan nearly dropped the cash box as feelings of shock and instant jealousy surged through him. His mouth dropped open in astonishment.

"Not cool." Bryan turned to face the voice beside him. It was Ross. Bryan wasn't sure how to respond. "He's your boyfriend, isn't he?" Ross asked. "You're a pretty serious couple."

"Uh, yeah… I thought so."

"Well, I guess it's okay to have an open relationship like that, as long as you both agree to it."

Bryan gulped. He didn't want to engage Ross or even reply to his comments. It really wasn't any of his business.

"I'm sure James was just messing around," Bryan said. "It's no big deal."

"If you say so." Ross smiled. "You know, Ian and I really *do* have an open relationship. You should call me sometime." He unzipped the bag and removed a dollar bill and an ink pen. He scribbled his phone number on it and held it out to Bryan. "Don't worry. They'll never miss a dollar." He winked, then turned, pulled open the door, and stepped inside.

Bryan shook his head and then glanced down at the bill. He quickly opened his cash box and tossed it inside. Hell would freeze over before he called an asshole like that.

"What was that all about?" Greg said. He'd approached from behind and was standing next to Bryan.

"Uh, I was gonna ask you the same thing."

"What're you talking about?" Greg's voice had an edge to it, as if he were pissed, which was extremely annoying to Bryan. What right did *he* have to be angry when he was the one out there getting felt up on the lawn?

"I saw what James did, how he groped you."

Greg pshawed. "Whatever. He was just messin'."

"Yeah, right...." Bryan turned away, but Greg grabbed his shoulder and spun him around. "Look, I told him it wasn't cool, and he backed off. But what was that shit with Ross?"

"It was nothing."

"Then what'd he give you? I saw him hand you something, and you shoved it in that box."

"It was a dollar." Bryan's temper flared. He didn't like being interrogated like that, especially when he'd done nothing wrong. "It was a dollar with his phone number on it!" He flipped open the box and pulled out the dollar, which was right on top. "Here, take it! He says he and Ian have an open relationship, so maybe you should give them a call." He tossed the dollar back into the box, then thrust the whole thing into Greg's arms. "Take the money inside. I'm out of here!"

He dashed as fast he could across the lawn, not looking back, then bolted down the sidewalk. Greg was calling his name, but he ignored everything and just kept running.

As the fury and embarrassment washed over him, his eyes filled with hot tears, and adrenaline pumped through his veins. He pushed himself, determined to run as fast as he could. Down the sidewalk he continued, passing pedestrians along the way. He didn't stop for anything.

Ten minutes later, when he finally felt his pounding heart was going to beat right out of his chest, he slowed his pace, then slowed even further till he was walking. At last he came to a stop and leaned forward, breathless. He bent over, grasping his knees with each of his palms.

"Fuck!" he screamed.

He was so pissed—enraged. He should have known something was up with James. He'd seen Greg flirting with him at Busch Gardens, but he'd given Greg the benefit of the doubt. Now today, James was groping him right there on the lawn, like it was no big deal. His emotions were so strung out, he couldn't tell if he was more angry or hurt. Devastated. He was utterly devastated.

Then it dawned on him how stupid he'd been to run away. He didn't even have his wallet or cell phone. He'd locked them in Greg's car. He had no choice but to go back to the center. It was his only option since he didn't really even know his way around the city, and even if he did, he had no money.

Defeated, he sat down on the curb along the edge of the road. Maybe Trevor or Adam would come looking for him. Or maybe Greg. Honestly he hoped not. He had no idea what he'd even say to Greg right now.

Something in the back of his mind told him to calm down and be rational. Maybe it was those damn counseling sessions; they were finally starting to get to him. It was like he could hear Hank talking in his head, urging him to identify the distortions of his thinking. No! This wasn't a distortion. This was something he'd seen with his own eyes. He'd seen James reach down and squeeze Greg's ass.

But then, Greg had seen Ross making a pass at him. He'd seen Bryan accept the dollar bill from him, taking his phone number. And Greg had jumped to conclusions. The way he'd fired questions at Bryan with his accusatory tone told Bryan exactly how little Greg trusted him. *Did I do the same thing? Did I jump to conclusions about something I saw?*

Greg had said James was just messin'. Horsing around, getting grab-assy. Wasn't that somewhat typical behavior of a horny college-aged gay guy? When Bryan went with Greg to the frat parties and to the youth group events, he'd witnessed a lot of that silliness. Guys were constantly grabbing each other, flirting, firing suggestive comments back and forth laced with sexual innuendo.

After all, they'd all been a bit randy, every single one of them flitting around that lawn wearing next to nothing and twerking their asses for the whole neighborhood to see. Bryan had laughed his ass off about it, and on more than one occasion he'd seen things—actions, body parts, gestures—that had stirred something within him. He'd gotten rock hard looking at all those bare chests, narrow waists, and tight, sexy, washboard abs.

So why was he being so childish? Why had he gotten jealous and then run away like a little kid?

He had to go back. He had to find Greg and apologize for being such a baby. Grown men didn't take off running in a fit of rage when they were upset. It was time for Bryan to man up.

He wiped his tear-streaked face with his palms, then pushed himself up from the curb. He hoped Greg would forgive him. He'd tell him how sorry he was and admit he was wrong for not trusting Greg. He'd tell him he was being a dick… then he'd offer to *suck* Greg's dick. He smiled at the thought. *Makeup sex!*

Just then, a black car, an SUV, drove by. It slowed, then stopped. Bryan watched as it did a U-turn, then pulled up alongside Bryan and stopped. He didn't recognize the car, and the windows were tinted. When the driver's window descended, he saw who it was: Ross.

"Hey, man, you all right?"

No, he wasn't all right, thanks to *him!* Bryan didn't say that, though. Instead he just nodded.

"You need a ride somewhere?"

"Uh, no. I'm just heading back to the Pride Center."

"You sure?" Ross said. "Everybody's gone. They all cleared out."

"Um, it's okay. I left my phone there."

"Well, hop in and I'll give you a lift."

There was no way he was getting into that car. Greg was already pissed that Ross had made a pass at him, and the last thing he wanted was for him to find out Bryan had gone for a ride with him in his SUV.

"I can walk."

"Dude, don't be silly. Look, I don't bite, and I promise I'll be a perfect gentleman. I get that you and Greg have this commitment thing, and that's cool. I didn't mean to start any problems for you."

"Well, you kinda did," Bryan said. He was scowling, and it was all he could do to even remain civil to this guy. "I don't need a ride from you. I can walk. I'll walk all the way home if I have to."

The smile on Ross's face quickly faded, and he reached up to remove his sunglasses. As he did so, Bryan noticed the steely expression on his face. He sensed Ross's anger and rage just from the look in his eyes.

Just then, the back door of his vehicle opened, and one of the big muscular guys who'd been on Ian's car wash team stepped out. The door on the passenger side opened at the same time, and Ian emerged.

"You mouthy little fucker," Ross spat. "I *said* I'll give you a fucking ride! Get him!"

Ian and the Goliath-sized jock charged toward him. Shocked and instantly terrified, he bolted, running as fast as he could back down the street toward the Pride Center. He heard shouting behind him and tires squealing, but he didn't look back. He leapt up onto the sidewalk and booked it at breakneck speed.

But he was already winded, tired from his first run, and the adrenaline that surged through him didn't help much. All of a sudden, he felt a blow to his back, and his feet went out from under him. He sailed through the air out onto the pavement, back into the middle of the road. He held his hands out and landed hard, scraping the skin off his palms and knees, then tumbled and hit the back of his head on the asphalt.

"Ahhh!" he cried out.

When he looked up, all he could see were the tires of Ross's sport utility vehicle. The Incredible Hulk man leaned over him, grabbed him roughly by the shirt, and tossed him into the backseat.

"Let me go!" Bryan protested. "You motherfuckers!"

CHAPTER
— 17 —

THE BACKSEAT wasn't spacious to begin with, and He-Man took up more than half of it. Bruised and bleeding, Bryan slid as far away from the brute as he could, hugging the passenger door.

"Don't even think of opening that door," Ross warned him.

"Go ahead, open it." Ian laughed from the front passenger seat. "We're only going sixty-five."

"What do you guys want?" Bryan responded. His reply came out more like a moan. "Where are you taking me?"

"Oh, what was I thinking?" Ross said, his voice dripping with sarcasm. "I'm not very polite sometimes. I forgot to introduce you to our friend. This here is Charlie. Some people affectionately refer to him as the Fridge."

Bryan glanced over at him and had no question where that nickname came from. He was a tank, and he reminded Bryan of those oversized wrestling guys with the massive, grotesquely exaggerated torsos. Bryan had always said that bodybuilding was a double-edged sword. When taken to extremes, it became hideous. Guys like the Fridge did not appeal to him in the least.

"Charlie's a real good friend. We've known each other for years, and he doesn't like it much when people mess with me. Ain't that right, Charlie?"

"That's right, boss," he mumbled in a baritone voice that seemed perfectly suited to his Neanderthal body. The dude was a troglodyte.

"Ross, stop this car and let me out! What you're doing here is a crime. It's kidnapping!"

The three of them laughed, and Ian spun around in his seat to look directly into Bryan's face. "Oh, dude, you're pretty messed up. Bleeding all over the place. I think you might need medical attention."

"That's right," Ross said. "We couldn't just leave you lying there on the street."

"What are you talking about? You're the ones who did this to me!"

Ross shook his head, grinning. "He's delusional, I think. Sayin' all kinds of shit that makes no sense."

"Greg's gonna come looking for me, and when he doesn't find me, he'll call the police."

"Greg's not gonna do shit." Ross was no longer grinning. He suddenly appeared furious, perhaps due to the mention of Greg's name. "Your goody-two-shoes boyfriend already dumped your ass like a hot potato. He's with his new fuck buddy now. They left together."

"You're lying! Greg wouldn't do—"

Charlie's backhand whacked Bryan square in the mouth before he could finish his sentence. "Mouthy little fucker," Charlie grumbled.

Bryan cried out as searing pain shot through his jaw. He cowered back into the corner, leaning his head against the window. He tasted blood in his mouth, and he was seeing stars. Closing his eyes, he prayed this all was just some sort of horrible nightmare.

He had to somehow get away from them. When the car stopped, he was going to have to try making a run for it again. But that was easier said than done. The Fridge was only inches from him, and he could easily hold Bryan in place. What were they going to do to him? Where were they taking him?

If only he hadn't run from Greg. If only he'd been mature enough to explain himself to Greg without flying off the handle, none of this would have happened. He wasn't supposed to be here now, locked in this car with these three thugs. He was supposed to be with Greg, celebrating an awesome day. If only there were some way to go back and undo his behavior. But there wasn't, and now he was trapped, totally at the mercy of a psychopath.

AS BRYAN sat there, staring out the window, panic began to set in. His head was throbbing. His bloody palms and knees stung from the pain of having skin ripped away when he'd landed on the asphalt. And now his tender jaw ached. It didn't seem any of his teeth had been loosened, but he must've cut the inside of his lip when the Fridge decked him.

None of that mattered, though. The physical pain was nothing compared to the anxiety he was experiencing as he wondered what was in store for him. He was a prisoner, locked in this car with three lunatics. And God only knew what the fuck they were planning for him. They were probably planning to take him to a remote area and beat the crap out of him… leave him for dead, or worse.

Bryan knew Ian was a rotten person. He'd known it since the day he'd badmouthed Greg and tried to turn Bryan against him. When his plan hadn't succeeded, he'd obviously been gunning for revenge. Ian probably also wasn't happy about Greg beating his boyfriend in the tennis tournament. What better way to get even than to fuck up Greg's boyfriend?

"Oh, by the way," Ross said casually. "You guys raised about thirty-five hundred bucks today. Our team raked in over two grand, but then we weren't out there slutting around like a bunch of bitches and hoes."

Wow! They'd raised that much? Bryan was surprised to hear it. If he weren't in his present situation, it would be a cause for celebration. He wondered how much the girls' team had earned.

"Ross…." Bryan was going to try one more time to reason with him. If he was tactful, perhaps he could talk some sense in him. "If you'll just stop and let me out, I promise I won't tell anyone. I won't say a word, but will just walk home and forget this ever happened."

Ian cracked up. "You wish! Just shut the fuck up."

Ross reached over and squeezed Ian's shoulder. "Don't let him rile you, babe. You'll have your revenge."

Revenge! Bryan had been right, that's what this was all about. It was some sort of scheme to get even with him. But for what, exactly?

"Excuse me, but can you explain this to me? What do you have to take revenge for? What'd I ever do to you?"

Ian spun in his seat and turned around to face Bryan. "You have a lot of fucking nerve. You show up out of nowhere, steal my boyfriend, try to get me fired from my job, and then you and Greg cheat at the tennis tournament and steal Ross's trophy! And you sit there like that and fucking ask me *what* you've ever done to me? I ought to beat the fuckin' shit out of you right now!"

Bryan's sore jaw dropped open. Astonished, he didn't even know how to respond. Ian was the one who was delusional. Every word from his mouth had been pure fantasy, almost like he was existing in a parallel universe.

"Ian, none of that's true."

"Shut up! Shut the fuck up!"

Bryan turned away and stared out the window. He had no idea where they were. He didn't recognize anything, but they didn't seem to be in a bad neighborhood. It looked more like an upscale suburb. He tried to memorize the businesses they passed and looked for noteworthy landmarks. He had to figure out a way to get out of his predicament. He had to think, and think fast. He'd heard somewhere that when an abduction occurred, the real crime almost always occurred at a secondary location. If the victim didn't escape before reaching that location, he rarely did at all.

As the car slowed, Bryan realized Ross was turning onto a side street. He saw a sign: Crystal Circle Drive. They pulled into the driveway of a condo, and Bryan looked above the garage at the house number: 2051. He reached for the door handle, and as he wrapped his fingers around it, he felt the firm grip of the Fridge's hand wrap around his bicep. Fuck! He couldn't do it. He couldn't free himself.

Ross pulled the car into the garage, then depressed the garage door remote, sealing them inside.

"Ross, please! Please don't do this!"

"Bring him inside, Charlie," Ross said as he pushed his door open. He acted like Bryan was nothing more than a bag of groceries.

As soon as Bryan's feet hit the concrete floor of the garage, he began screaming. "Help! Someone help me!"

Charlie's big fist connected with the back of his head, sending him lurching forward. "Shut up and quit your wailin'!" He wrapped one of his paws around the nape of Bryan's neck, and with his other hand, he grabbed Bryan's arm and twisted it painfully behind his back. He marched Bryan forward, toward the entrance of the condo.

Once inside, Bryan glanced around. The luxurious surroundings were unbefitting a crime scene. This was a real nice place. Expensive. He wondered if it belonged to Ross or to Ian. Ross answered his unspoken question.

"Welcome to my crib, bitchboy." His laughter was insidious, and when Ian joined in, they reminded Bryan of evil characters from a really bad B-grade movie. This whole thing was fucked up. Stuff like this didn't happen in real life. "Take him downstairs, Charlie. We'll be down in a minute."

"No problem, boss." Why the hell was this guy calling Ross "boss"? Was he some sort of a mafia kingpin or something? Charlie didn't seem too swift, though. Bryan thought he might have about two functioning brain cells. Steroids would do that to a person, he surmised.

Bryan had no choice but to go where Charlie took him. The behemoth-sized oaf had Bryan firmly in his grip and wasn't letting go. He pushed Bryan down a hallway, then instructed him to open the door in front of him. Bryan did so and saw it led to a staircase. "You can either walk down, or I can throw you down. Your choice."

Bryan walked.

His heart was beating rapidly in his chest as Charlie thrust Bryan into one of the leather chairs. "Sit there and don't move," he ordered. "I swear to God, if you move one inch, I'll crush your nuts." The Fridge plopped down beside him in an adjacent recliner.

As Bryan sat there, he kept telling himself this couldn't be real. It was too twisted for cable TV, and it all had to be some sort of joke. The whole thing was a fucked-up practical joke, and Ian was going to come downstairs at any second and tell him it was all a staged prank.

Please, God, get me out of this. Please!

Charlie just sat there, staring straight ahead. He didn't turn on the television or make any effort to converse. He didn't do anything other than sit there and stare. The guy really was a fridge. A walking, breathing appliance.

It was when he heard the footsteps on the staircase that Bryan really began to panic. He turned and saw Ross and Ian standing at the foot of the stairwell. Ian was holding a belt in his hand, and Ross was shirtless.

"Shall we get this show on the road?" Ross said.

Bryan's eyes grew wide with fear, and then he bolted from the chair, charging toward them in a last-ditch effort to escape. It was pointless, though. He was easily tackled, and as he felt the smooth leather of the belt wrap around his neck, he knew he was fucked.

And then he was. Literally.

HE DIDN'T know exactly what time it was, somewhere in the wee hours of the morning, around the time the bars closed. They dropped him off downtown in a section of the city Bryan didn't recognize. When Ross pulled the car up to the curb and ordered Bryan out, he didn't think he'd heard correctly. He was sure they were taking him somewhere to kill him. A part of him wished they had.

Right now, though, he was numb. He'd screamed and cried to the point where he had no voice left. They'd stuffed something in his mouth so they wouldn't have to hear him beg them to stop. That is, except for when they decided to use his mouth for their own purposes.

He'd been beaten, strangled, and violated in every conceivable way. He was bruised and sore, and he barely had the energy to push the door open. Somehow he managed, and after a forceful shove to the center of his back from Charlie, Bryan stumbled out of the car and onto the curb.

"We'll have to do this again sometime," Ross said sarcastically. "You were a blast!"

Fuck you! Bryan didn't say anything out loud. He just crumpled to his knees as the door slammed behind him and the car sped away.

He didn't know how long he was there, lying on the pavement, before he heard voices. He didn't care. He didn't care who saw him or what they did to him at this point. What worse could possibly happen to him than what he'd already been through?

"Dude, you're fucked up," someone said.

"Who *is* that?" another voice said.

"Some twink coked out his head on meth, probably. Just leave him...."

"No, wait."

Bryan heard the young man approach him. He opened his eyes and looked up. It was a kid about Bryan's age, wearing lots of jewelry. "Hon, are you okay? What happened to you?"

"Ty, he's stoned. Just leave him; he's not our problem."

"Brandon, we can't leave him. He could die!"

Bryan glanced over to the one named Brandon. They must be a couple. "Help me," Bryan managed to whisper.

"I'm calling 911," Ty announced.

"No, Tyler! You don't wanna get the police down here. Look, it's not our fault this junkie ODed. We can't do anything for him...."

"Brandon!" Tyler knelt beside Bryan. "Oh my God, he's bleeding. Someone hit him. Hey, can you tell us what happened?"

Bryan tried to speak. "Call...."

"You want me to call someone for you?"

Bryan nodded. "Greg."

Tyler was already holding his phone. "Do you remember his number?"

He held the screen up for Bryan, and Bryan tried his best to focus. As he reached out to touch the buttons, his hand began to shake. Tyler slipped behind him and cradled Bryan's body with his lap. "You're okay," he said soothingly. "Take your time."

At last he was able to type in the digits. He slumped backward as Tyler pulled the phone away.

"What's your name?" Tyler whispered.

"Bry... an."

"Hello? Hello, is this Greg? ... Hey, we have a friend of yours here, I think he says his name is Bryan. He's really bad. Stoned or drunk or something. He's passed out on the sidewalk. ... I don't know, man. We don't wanna leave him. ... We're down by the Body Shop." It must've been the name of a bar. Bryan heard Tyler giving Greg an address.

His world faded to black.

CHAPTER
— 18 —

SILENT TEARS streamed down Bryan's cheeks as Greg scooped him up. "Baby, what'd you do? What the fuck did you do to yourself?"

It was a good question. Bryan couldn't say it. He couldn't tell Greg what had happened. He couldn't put into words all he'd been through.

"Why'd you run away?"

Bryan shook his head, unable to speak.

"Your lip is bleeding. Did you fall? And oh my God, your hands, they're all scraped up. And your legs! Bryan, I'm taking you to the emergency room."

"No!" he cried. "Please…."

Greg carried Bryan over to the car and strapped him into the passenger seat. "Were you drinking?" he whispered. Bryan shook his head. "Well, you're okay now. I'm here. Just sit tight, and I'll be right back."

"Don't leave me!" Bryan sobbed.

"Oh baby, what happened to you?"

"I… uh… uh… I'm so sorry!"

"No, no, no! It was all my fault. I've been fucking frantic, looking for you. So have Trevor and Adam… and their dads."

A sob escaped Bryan's throat. "No, please don't… don't tell them!" He was so mortified. So ashamed.

Greg continued to crouch beside the passenger door. Tyler and Brandon were standing behind him. "Okay, okay," he said soothingly.

"You're all right now. Just let me get you home. I'm just going to close the door and walk around to the driver's side. You're safe now." He leaned in and kissed the side of Bryan's tear-streaked face.

He about lost it again when Greg at last pulled away.

"Thank you guys so much for calling, and for staying with him. Here, please take this." He must have been offering them money.

"No, man, it's cool," Tyler replied.

"Take it," Brandon said.

Bryan didn't hear any more of the exchange because Greg closed the door.

When Greg climbed in behind the wheel, he immediately reached out and took hold of Bryan's hand. "Baby, something happened to you. You're really messed up." He squeezed Bryan's hand, then released it to shift the car into gear. "But I'm so glad I found you. I was so wrong earlier. I should have trusted you. I know Ross was just pulling shit."

"Ross!" The name was like a knife in Bryan's chest.

"Did… did Ross do something?" Greg said, the pitch of his voice escalating. "Bryan, tell me what happened."

"They… they…."

"They? There were more than one? Did Ross and Ian do something? Oh fuck!"

"And… the other one." Bryan looked out the window, and suddenly realized he was no longer in his own body. At least it didn't feel like it. It felt as if he was watching himself from afar and this whole scene was make-believe. "The other one," he whispered, "was the worst."

He couldn't turn to face Greg, but he heard him. He was making a call. "I've got him, and we're on our way. I'll meet you there." Bryan didn't know where Greg was taking him, but he was too exhausted to argue with him. He closed his eyes and drifted off to sleep.

THE POLICE officer stood beside Bryan's hospital bed, talking to Jeff and Greg. "Obviously he's been assaulted, but if he can't tell us anything, there's nothing I can do."

"Sir, I told you, it was Ross and Ian," Greg said.

"*He* has to tell me. Otherwise, I have no reason to believe a crime was committed."

Bryan couldn't. He couldn't talk about it right now. He couldn't repeat what had been done to him, but when the medical personnel had examined him, probing every inch of his body, they'd discovered the evidence. There was no question he'd been violated, and judging from the bruises on his neck, arms, thighs, and back, he'd been brutalized severely. Worst of all was when they'd examined his private region.

"He's torn open!" Jeff was practically screaming. "Whatever the hell happened, it was not consensual. You've got to do something!"

"Sir, with all due respect, he was in the gay district, outside the bar. How do we know…?"

Greg dropped to his knees beside the bed and grabbed hold of Bryan's hand. "Babe, please… please tell us. I know it's hard. But please try… for me."

Slowly Bryan nodded, and before he could even speak, the waterworks started again. Tears streamed down his cheeks, and he'd be damned if he could make them stop. He didn't even know at this point why he was crying. He could make no sense of his emotions. There was a gaping hole inside his chest, an emptiness, and his entire world was overshadowed with gray.

"Ian and Ross, and they had a friend… his name was Charlie."

Greg squeezed his hand.

"These are the guys you were with tonight?" the officer asked.

Bryan nodded. "They picked me up, tried to offer me a ride." As he began to speak it got easier; the words started to flow from his mouth. He wasn't feeling what he was saying. He was just telling. Like a robot, he was reciting facts, recalling what had happened.

"Ross was nice at first. He offered to take me home with him, but I said no. Then he offered to give me a ride back to the Pride Center. When I said no again, the other guys jumped out of the car and chased me.

"Honest, I tried to get away. I ran as fast as I could, but I was tired, and the big one tackled me."

"Oh my God." Greg was now crying.

"Go on," the officer said. "Then what happened?"

"They got me in the car, and I couldn't get out. The big one named Charlie had a hold of me. We were in the backseat. I argued, yelled at Ross, and demanded he let me out. Charlie hit me, and at first I thought he broke my jaw."

"Do you need to hear any more?" Jeff was on the other side of the bed, rubbing Bryan's arm. "Officer, can you *please* go arrest these thugs now?"

The police officer held up his hand. "Go on. What happened next? I know this is difficult."

Surprisingly, it really wasn't all that difficult, not anymore. Once he started talking, the words just seemed to slip out of his mouth on their own. Bryan was no longer feeling anything. He was telling the story as if it had happened to someone else.

"I tried to figure out where they were taking me, but I was lost. I didn't know the area, but I looked out the window for landmarks. We passed a train station, and there was a big sign that had a cowboy on it. Eventually we were out of the business district in a really nice area with expensive-looking houses. They took me to a condo."

"Sir, I know where he's talking about. It's Ian's neighborhood...."

"Did you notice the number on the condo?"

He had no idea how he remembered, but he did. "2051 Crystal Circle Drive," he whispered. "I tried again to run, but the big one grabbed me by the neck, dragged me inside, and took me downstairs to the basement. Ian and Ross came down a few minutes later. They had a belt they wrapped around my neck. They pulled it tight so it strangled me. I tried to breathe. I tried to fight!" He was getting excited, and the emotion was returning to his voice. Overwhelmed, he sobbed.

"Oh my God!" Greg leaned in and kissed his temple, still holding his hand tightly. "Bryan, I'm so sorry. I'm so sorry."

"They tore off my clothes. I swear to you, they forced me. I swear, Greg... I fucking swear!" Greg was crying openly now as Bryan looked into his eyes. "Will you forgive me?" Bryan whispered.

"Bryan, baby... oh God. There's nothing to forgive."

The officer took a step closer to the foot of the bed. "I'm sorry. I know this is difficult. I know these details are hard to talk about...."

"They forced me. All three of them. Anal and oral." With that confession, Bryan's face twisted with anguish and he released a gut-wrenching sob. He pulled his hand free from Greg's grasp and covered his face, convulsing uncontrollably. The horror of it all flooded his memory as he wept. He couldn't seem to stop. He couldn't do anything other than cry and try as best he could to breathe.

"I'm calling the DA and we'll get a warrant issued. We'll have them in custody before daybreak." The officer reached down and touched Bryan's ankle. "I'm sorry to put you through this, but we'll do everything we can. Someone from the prosecutor's office will be here shortly."

"Thank you, Officer," Jeff said. He followed him outside as Bryan continued to lie crying on the bed.

He lowered his hands from his face, and Greg reached up to wipe away his tears. "Shh," he said, "you're okay now. I'm right here."

"Greg, I'm so sorry," Bryan whispered.

"No… no, please don't be sorry. It wasn't your fault."

Why did Bryan feel like it was, though?

"I'VE GOT to be honest with you," the middle-aged woman said. Her hair was pulled back tightly in a bun, and she sat in the hospital chair with her legs crossed. "This is going to be a difficult case to prosecute."

Jeff was pacing the room, running his hands through his hair. "I'm sorry, but I just don't get it. How can you say this is difficult to prosecute? There were three of them, and they kidnapped and raped him!"

"Sir, I understand how you feel. Believe me, I do. But right now it's just a matter of their word against Bryan's. We've brought them in for questioning, and they all tell the same story. They say they hooked up and went back to Ross's condo, that Bryan went willingly and the encounter was consensual."

"Obviously, that's not true," Greg said. "He has bruises, and they tore him open! And they left him alongside the street afterward."

"They claim he begged them to be rough, that it was a sexual fantasy. Then they took him back to the bar, and he was fine when they left him." She crossed her arms over her chest. "The part of the story that is most difficult is that they brought him back to the bar. If they'd raped and assaulted him, why would they do that?"

"To make it look like they hadn't kidnapped him!" Jeff shouted. "My God, this isn't rocket science!"

The prosecutor took a deep breath, then pushed herself up from her chair. "Sir, I understand why you're angry. This is really heartbreaking, but I just don't see how we can bring this case to trial without any witnesses."

"Wait!" Greg said. "Maybe there *are* some witnesses. Maybe someone saw when they abducted him."

She nodded. "We've thought of that, and we have officers canvassing that neighborhood to see if anyone saw anything. I'll be blunt, though. If we don't come up with a smoking gun, this case is dead in the water. As much as I hate to tell you this, the three of them are going to walk."

CHAPTER

— 19 —

BRYAN WAS only in the hospital overnight. There was no medical reason to keep him, but mentally and emotionally, he was still in bad shape. Jeff had called Hank and told him about the tragedy, and Hank dropped everything and rushed to the hospital to be by Bryan's side that morning of his release.

Bryan really didn't care, though. He had no desire to talk to Hank. Like all the other authority figures, Hank wasn't likely to believe Bryan's version of what had happened. Even the police officer who'd originally taken Bryan's statement came back after questioning Ross and more or less accused Bryan of lying. Well, that was the impression Bryan got, anyway.

And the prosecutor had been no better. She'd said it was a matter of Bryan's word against the other three guys. In other words, she didn't believe Bryan. He wished now that he had never told.

His biggest concern wasn't whether or not they got away with it. Bryan hated them, and he wished all three of them would get what they had coming to them, but that was far less important to him than his relationship with Greg. What did Greg think of him now? Did he believe Bryan? How could he?

The one person who did seem to believe Bryan implicitly was Jeff. That was probably due to the fact that Jeff was just an overly trusting person. Of course he'd take Bryan's word for it. Of course he'd support Bryan, even when it wasn't logical or popular. But Bryan couldn't expect Greg to be so naïve.

The whole situation saddened Bryan because he really was telling the truth, but it was a truth that was stranger than fiction. He felt as if his entire world had suddenly come to a screeching halt. He was again engulfed in a sea of depression, and all he wanted to do was cry.

When Bryan got home that Sunday afternoon, Greg remained with him at the house, and they lay down together on Bryan's bed. He curled up into Greg's strong embrace and snuggled. Just to feel his strength and protection, to smell him and bask in the warmth of his body heat, was a comfort to his soul. But it wasn't enough to erase the gaping hole inside him. It wasn't enough to right everything that was now so very wrong.

"I love you," Greg whispered.

"I know," Bryan replied. *But why?*

Why did Greg still love him? How could he? Bryan had surrendered to the advances of those despicable cretins. He'd allowed himself to be violated in the worst possible way. How could Greg still feel the same way about him?

Bryan didn't feel the same way about himself. He'd been making progress; his life had gotten so much better. He loved his new family, his job, and even his classes at school. And he had the most wonderful, amazing, and incredibly hot boyfriend in the whole world. But now… it all seemed so phony.

"Greg, do you believe me?" Bryan's voice was barely audible.

"Of course I believe you."

"Really? Nobody else does."

Greg placed his hand on Bryan's shoulder and pulled him toward himself. They were spooning, and Greg repositioned Bryan so he was now lying flat on his back, looking up into Greg's face. "That's not true. We all believe you… we *know* you aren't lying."

"How do you know?" He hated the fact he was crying again, but the tears seemed to come on their own, and he couldn't stop them. "That prosecutor lady said it was their word against mine."

"Yeah, well, I was there. I saw you right after it happened. I know you weren't fucking lying, and if anyone says you were, I'll fucking kick their ass."

"I don't wanna go back to work. How can I?"

"You don't have to, at least not while he's there." Greg was referring to Ian, but it was as if he didn't want to even so much as speak his name.

"I'll have to find a new job."

"When you're ready…."

Would he ever be ready? How would he start his life over after something like this? How would he ever find the strength?

STARTING OVER sucked. Bryan discovered it wasn't just a matter of putting the incident behind him. If that had been all there was to it, it would've been fairly easy. The shit that had happened to him that day was something he'd love to forget. He'd love to bury it, pretend like it never occurred.

But starting over meant healing, and to heal he had to acknowledge everything he was feeling. He had to talk about his assault in far more graphic detail than he was comfortable with. He had to decide he was stronger than this tragedy.

Baby steps. That was how he coped, by taking things one day at a time. He did quit his job, and instead focused on school. It sounded lame, but making it through a day felt like a huge accomplishment to him. He struggled to remain focused in class, and at times he'd become emotional or angry. He relied on Greg probably far more than he should.

And Greg never left his side. He stayed over several nights a week, and on the nights he did not stay at Bryan's house, Bryan went to Greg's. Mostly they cuddled, and Greg held him, told him how beautiful he was and how much he loved him. He never pressured Bryan to make love.

Then one day, the week of Christmas, Bryan told him he was ready. He wanted to try, anyway, and so they made love. Bryan's biggest fear had been that he'd have flashbacks, that the memories of his rape would invade his mind every time he was intimate with Greg. Thankfully, this did not prove to be the case. It was the opposite, in fact. Being physically intimate with Greg was an incredible, nearly miraculous escape. Those moments of ecstasy proved to be the times he was 100 percent free of the haunting memories.

As a result, he became insatiable. He wanted to do it all the time.

In spite of all that had happened, the Christmas holiday was wonderful. Jeff hosted a huge Christmas dinner, and Bryan received tons of presents, far more than he'd ever gotten back in Michigan. Of course, Greg was included. That afternoon they went to visit Allison, and they stayed and talked for hours. Bryan was tickled to receive a scarf from her, though he wasn't sure when he'd get to use it.

"Greg's just gonna have to take me on a ski vacation," he joked.

"Well, I figured you'd be going home to visit your family in Michigan," she said. Bryan hadn't told her he was estranged from his parents.

Two days later, a package arrived from Bryan's folks, a belated Christmas gift, perhaps. Maybe they were starting to come around. Bryan tore into the box and eagerly unpacked it.

A bible and a stack of literature about how to be cured of homosexuality.

Furious, he stood up and hurled the Bible across the room. It collided with one of Jeff's decorative wall hangings, and seconds later, Jeff came charging into the room. "Oh my God, Bryan, what was that? Are you all right?"

Bryan slunk down into one of the living room chairs, burying his face into his palms. He shook his head and began to sob.

Jeff knelt beside him and held him. He didn't say a word about the damage to the artwork.

ONE SATURDAY morning in mid-January, Bryan woke up early, unable to sleep any longer, and decided to tackle the remainder of a research paper he'd been working on. He padded his way to the bathroom and then downstairs to the kitchen, where he started a pot of coffee. He never thought he'd see the day when he'd be the first person up in the house, even beating Jeff to the kitchen. But his sleep had been all fucked up for the past month. Falling asleep wasn't easy; he'd usually toss and turn, lie awake with thoughts constantly racing through his head. Flashbacks plagued him, not just of the assault, but of his life in general. He'd recall incidents from his childhood where he'd done stupid things, things that were mean to others or just plain ignorant. Then he'd tell himself, "I'm being punished."

If he truly believed in karma, how could he deny that he'd gotten what was coming to him? For all those years he'd been the world's biggest homophobe. He'd bullied Noah, Evan's boyfriend, but Noah hadn't been his only victim. There'd been a lot of other kids he'd picked on, tormented, and pushed around. The last half of his senior year, after he witnessed what Jeff and Brett did when they single-handedly saved the school's drama department with their generous donation, Bryan had tried to change. He'd turned over a new leaf and even went out of his way to stick up for the kids who were being abused or bullied. But was it too little, too late?

And then when he did finally doze off, his sleep was fitful. He'd wake up after an hour or so, terrified. The bedsheets would be soaked with sweat, and his heart would pound so hard in his chest he thought it would explode. Those were the times he knew he'd been dreaming. He knew it not by recalling the specifics of the dream itself, but by the feelings. The fear, the dread, the spine-tingling terror made him a little shaky, and he'd suddenly realize he was crying, but he didn't know exactly why.

He did, on occasion have vivid flashbacks. They didn't play in his head like a movie reel, though. They were mere glimpses. He'd recall something specific—a thought that had passed through his mind while they were raping him. Or a mental image of Ian's face twisted into a sadistic grin. He'd remember the smell, the color of the carpeting, the big ugly recliner on the opposite side of the room. All these minor, inconsequential details created a mosaic in his mind, a puzzle he'd rather not complete. But as the memories surfaced and the images flashed into his mind, he was reminded of the big picture.

So he didn't sleep well, and by default was becoming more and more a morning person, though not in the sense Trevor and Jeff were. They were cheerful morning people; Bryan was what he'd call "functional." He didn't bound out of bed and begin singing, eager to face all the challenges of a bright, new dawn. No, he wasn't Mary fucking Poppins. But if he could just drag his ass out of bed and focus on something, he'd be able to distract himself from the racing thoughts and intense emotions.

He stood by the coffee brewer, waiting for the carafe to fill up enough for him to get a single cup. That was when he remembered a conversation he'd had one morning with Liam, his ex-boyfriend. Liam was a coffee drinker, and Bryan had often teased him about it. Eighteen was too young, Bryan told him, to drink so much coffee. Coffee was an old people's beverage.

"Fuck that, I need the caffeine."

Bryan wondered what would have happened with him and Liam if things had been different. He really cared about his ex, and he harbored no bitterness or hatred toward him. Liam just hadn't been ready for a serious, long-term relationship. If Bryan were to be completely honest, he'd have to admit he hadn't been ready at that time either. They both were just beginning to find their way.

Liam had been the one who'd satisfied and fulfilled many of Bryan's fantasies. Liam was sexually adventurous, extremely open-minded when it came to kink. And he often liked it when Bryan would get rough with him.

Bryan's cheeks grew hot as he stared down at the black coffee dripping into the carafe. He recalled how Liam had wanted him to dominate, call him names, treat him like Bryan's little slut. And Liam had even suggested at one point that they try to arrange a three-way, so he could be topped from both ends. He'd wanted Bryan and another guy—Liam didn't even seem to care who that other hypothetical partner might be—to simultaneously dominate him.

At the time, Bryan had laughed and promised Liam he'd think about it. Now, as he stood there recalling that conversation, Bryan felt a bit sick to his stomach. How could he have even considered honoring such a request? How could he have ever been forceful or abusive to Liam—or to anyone he loved?

He closed his eyes, feeling queasy, and grabbed the counter to steady himself. Fuck, he was gonna lose it. He turned and dashed out of the kitchen, down the hall into the bathroom. He slid to his knees in front of the commode and began to retch. His entire body convulsed and continued to do so until there was nothing left inside him. Even then, the dry heaves continued.

A hand on his back offered reassurance, and Bryan knew immediately it was Jeff. With his other hand, Jeff held Bryan's head. "You're okay," he whispered. "Remember to breathe."

When at last the puking subsided, Bryan looked up into Jeff's face. Bryan gasped as he tried to take in as big a gulp of air as possible.

"Small breaths," Jeff said, his voice calm and soothing. He framed Bryan's face with his palms and looked into his eyes. "Breathe… slowly."

And finally he was able to do exactly that. As his breathing became more controlled, the urge to vomit subsided. "Thank… uh… thank you."

Jeff removed some toilet tissue from the dispenser and wiped Bryan's mouth. "Shh. Come here." He wrapped his arms around Bryan and pulled him in for a comforting hug. Bryan just melted, laying his head against Jeff's chest as Jeff sat there on the floor cradling him, stroking his hair. "You're okay now," Jeff whispered.

A few minutes later, when they returned to the kitchen, Bryan apologized. "I'm sorry, I don't know what came over me."

"When I was younger, I used to have episodes like that myself. I'd get upset about things and suddenly feel sick to my stomach. The doctor said it was nerves. I don't know… my mom called it a nervous stomach. I haven't gotten sick like that in years."

"Yeah, I guess that's what it was. Nerves."

"Bryan, what were you thinking about at the time?" They took a seat at the dining room table, next to each other. "Were you having a flashback?"

Bryan nodded. "Yeah, kind of. But probably not what you're thinking. I mean, it wasn't a flashback of what happened to me." He still found it difficult to say the word rape. "It was a memory of something from a while ago. Something with Liam, my ex."

Jeff didn't pressure him to go on, nor did he interrupt with questions. He simply waited, placing a hand atop Bryan's.

"See, Liam wasn't like me. He wasn't a jock, but he wasn't a nerd either. He was sort of a rebel. He smoked pot, had tattoos. He was the kind of guy who listened to really edgy music and wore really unpopular, unfashionable clothes. Emo, maybe, but not exactly.

"I guess you could say he was a rebel, and when it came to sex...." Bryan wasn't sure he could talk about this with Jeff.

"It's okay," Jeff said, smiling. "Go on."

Bryan laughed nervously, then smiled. "Well, sexually, he liked a lot of kinky stuff. I was pretty new to everything, and I wanted to experiment."

"Of course," Jeff nodded.

"Well, he liked some bondage and stuff. Nothing severe. I mean, he didn't want me to beat him or anything. But he liked when I got rough. He liked...." Bryan felt as if his cheeks were on fire. "He liked being spanked, and he wanted me to call him names and stuff, treat him like... um... like my slut, I guess."

"He was more comfortable in a sexually submissive role, and he wanted you to dominate him."

"Yeah. Right. And...." He felt the emotion surging again, and he really didn't want to start crying.

"And now, after what's happened to you, you feel guilty. You feel like the way you treated Liam sexually isn't all that different from what Ross and his friends did to you."

The tears did begin to flow, and Bryan nodded.

"Bryan, would it really surprise you much if I confessed to you that I'm a sexually submissive guy? I mean, without getting into graphic detail, I can assure you I much prefer being a bottom, and I can assure you, Brett prefers to top."

Bryan smiled through his tears. These guys were like parents to him, and he really didn't want to visualize it. Yet, what Jeff was saying made sense. If he'd had to guess, he'd definitely say Jeff seemed more like the type of guy who'd bottom.

"When Brett and I first met, I didn't understand any of that. I didn't know what a top or bottom was, and I sure didn't know anything about being sexually submissive or dominant. But I loved Brett, and he awakened in me a desire to explore that side of myself. I've heard people talk about it as BDSM. Some people think it's a lifestyle choice. Some say it's unhealthy and harmful.

"But as I was growing up, I felt inferior, not just because I was gay, but also because I had a genuine need to serve and be dominated by guys who were physically superior. And when I say that, I don't mean that Brett is superior to me as a person, but he has a body—or did have—worthy of worship."

Bryan laughed. "I can see where you'd say that. Look how Trevor is with Adam. Adam's got the studly body, but Trevor's cute too. So why can't they worship each other?"

"Oh, believe me, Brett made me feel very worshiped. And loved. But just as I craved submitting to him, he also loved dominating. It was all about fulfilling each other's needs.

"And when Liam expressed his fantasies to you, he wasn't asking you to abuse him. He was simply proposing a power exchange, one in which he trusted you to give him what he yearned for."

"I'm not sure Liam thought about it in those terms. I think he was just horny and wanted to get off, and the kinky side of him was into some unusual stuff."

"Whether you realize it or not, you and I just said the same exact thing in different words." Jeff laughed. "The point is, everything you did with Liam was consensual. Bryan, I don't judge other people and their sexual inclinations or preferences. You might reach a point in your life when you want to experiment with BDSM. You might enjoy submission or domination. You might like unusual scenes. Three-ways. Four-ways. Orgies. Whatever. I'm certainly not endorsing anything in particular. I'm not saying you should or should not explore a particular fetish. All I can say is that it always should be consensual and it always should be safe. And it's something you have to be able to discuss with your partner."

"Well, I don't want to do three-ways or anything like that. I love Greg, and that's enough for me. I think that sort of stuff would feel too much like cheating. Fuck, I feel like I've cheated already." He couldn't believe he just used the F word.

Jeff shook his head frantically. "No, Bryan! You did not cheat on Greg. What those guys did to you was not consensual. And you can say whatever you want about group sex, whether you agree or disagree with it. But that's not the issue here. Yeah, it might be a fantasy for some submissive guys to be dominated by three partners, but when it is nonconsensual, it's anything but a fantasy. It's a nightmare. It's *rape*!

"Bryan, please don't conflate two different things. Dominating a willing, consensual partner is not the same thing as rape. Not even close."

What Jeff was saying made sense. Bryan just had to start believing it.

CHAPTER
— **20** —

"THE THING that really bothers me is the fact that Greg kept working there with Ian." Bryan was in Hank's office, halfway through his counseling session. He felt he had to express his feelings, even though it was a sentiment he couldn't bring himself to share with Greg. "I don't know exactly what I expected. I mean, it's not reasonable for me to expect him to quit his job just because of me. And...." He was beginning to get choked up.

"And you thought maybe he'd beat the shit out of Ian and Ross?"

Yeah, to be honest, that was exactly what Bryan thought. Or at least now, in retrospect, it seemed to him that his boyfriend should have done something to defend his honor. "Hank, how could he go into work every day and work alongside someone who did something like that to the person he supposedly loves with all his heart?"

"Bryan," Hank said as he leaned forward in his chair, "you have to talk to Greg about this. You're not with him 24-7. How do you know he didn't do something to defend your honor? You don't know what type of exchange Greg had with Ian or Ross."

Bryan sighed. "I know, but you know what? I really just want to put this behind me now. It's been four months, and I have a new job. I have my own car, and school's going great. I was even thinking of maybe cutting back on the counseling sessions."

Hank nodded. "I was thinking the same thing myself."

"You were?" A wave of panic swept over Bryan. Was Hank ready to dump him?

Hank smiled. "Well, hold on. You're not getting rid of me that easily, but maybe we can go to biweekly sessions, meet every other week."

Bryan exhaled. "Yeah. Every other week sounds good." He couldn't believe how much his feelings about Hank had changed over the course of the spring semester. Since the rape, Hank had been his rock, and without him, Bryan wasn't sure how he'd have survived. Lord knew there'd been days when he was ready to call it quits. "I do have a confession to make, though."

Hank's eyebrows rose slightly. "Okay. I'm listening."

Bryan smiled sheepishly. "Back in December, around the time I was thinking of quitting our sessions altogether, I stopped taking my medication for a while."

Hank nodded slowly. "And now?"

"Well, after the rape, I was so depressed, and I started taking the pills again. I continued after you adjusted the dosage, and I've been on them ever since."

"Well, that's a good thing, Bryan. But I want to be clear about something. What happened to you was not a result of your decision to stop the meds."

Bryan wasn't so sure. "Maybe it was... indirectly. See, that day of the car wash, Greg and I had our first disagreement. We argued, and I was so pissed I took off. I just freaked out and ran, as fast as I could. Maybe if I'd been on the meds, I wouldn't have reacted that way."

"Maybe, but we'll never know. Honestly, I doubt antidepressants would have had any impact on how you reacted. They are not magic pills, Bryan. They aren't going to solve all your problems. You'll still get upset about things. There will be days when you'll feel sad. Emotions are part of our humanity, and it's perfectly normal for you to be freaked out after your first argument."

"But I acted like such a baby. It wasn't very mature of me to just take off like that...."

"And you're not the first nineteen-year-old to do something immature."

Bryan laughed, then nodded. "Yeah, I guess you're right."

"But in the future, I'd like to have a conversation with you before you decide to discontinue your medication."

"I know, I know."

"Bryan, I'm very proud of you," Hank said, and Bryan's heart swelled with warm affection. "What you've been through would be enough to set most people back considerably. You're a very strong person, and you should be proud of yourself."

This was one time Bryan was determined not to get teary-eyed. "I can't say I'm there yet, but I'm working on it."

Hank held up his arm and checked the time on his wristwatch. "Unless you have something further you'd like to discuss, why don't we plan on scheduling your next appointment in two weeks."

"Sounds great." Bryan pushed himself up from the chair as Hank stood and extended his hand. Bryan ignored it and moved closer to Hank, then wrapped him in a heartfelt embrace. "Thanks for everything, Hank."

Hank slapped him affectionately on the back as he returned the hug. "You're very welcome, Bryan."

OVER THE previous four months, Greg had been another rock of support, and Bryan had not said a word to him about his job at the country club. In fact, he hadn't discussed his feelings about it with anyone, but it troubled him. He tried putting himself in Greg's shoes and wondered what he'd do if their positions were reversed. If one of their coworkers had assaulted Greg, Bryan knew there'd be no way he could continue working with the person who'd perpetrated the crime. In fact, he'd kick the living shit out of them, regardless of the consequences.

So why hadn't Greg done the same? Why hadn't he defended Bryan's honor? Was it simply that he didn't want to risk losing his own job? Or was it that Greg didn't actually believe Bryan was telling the truth about what had happened?

Yet Bryan had no reason to doubt Greg's trust. He had assured Bryan that he believed him implicitly. And in the days and weeks following the assault, Greg had been there for Bryan. They'd slept together every night. Greg was the one who'd held him, comforted him, and reassured him that he'd get through this period of his life.

For Christmas Greg had gotten him a twenty-four karat gold necklace, three different types of cologne, some sexy underwear, and a subscription to *Sports Illustrated*. Their holiday together had been perfect. Then Valentine's Day had been even more amazing.

Hank was right. Bryan simply had to talk to Greg about it, express his feelings. Regardless of what Greg's reasoning was for keeping his job working alongside Ian, it had hurt Bryan. He owed it to Greg and to the future of their relationship to have the discussion. He decided to bite the bullet and engage Greg in the conversation as soon as he got home.

As he turned down the street to his home, Bryan noticed Greg's car in his drive, but thoughts of having a conversation with him instantly vanished. Parked behind Greg's car was a police vehicle. What was going on? Why were the police at his house?

He pulled up alongside the curb and got out, then rushed up to the porch. He hoped something wasn't wrong, and hesitated momentarily before taking hold of the door handle and entering the house. As he stepped inside, four pair of eyes turned to him. Jeff and Brett were sitting on the living room sofa, and Greg was seated on the loveseat adjacent to them. A uniformed officer, the same one who'd taken Bryan's statement in the hospital the night of the rape, sat in a chair across from Greg.

"Bryan," the officer said, "we've been waiting for you."

Bryan stepped into the living room and walked over to Greg. Greg extended his hand and Bryan reached out to take hold of it, then sat down beside him. "What's going on?"

"Bryan, I'm here to deliver news on your case. Good news."

"You found a witness?" Bryan leaned forward, eager to hear what the officer had to say.

The young, clean-cut policeman nodded. "Not only did we find a witness, but we also acquired some other evidence. The three men who assaulted you were taken into custody this morning and charged with multiple counts of rape and kidnapping."

Astonished, Bryan's mouth fell open. He felt his eyes brimming with tears. He'd all but abandoned hope of justice being served. "How?" was all he could manage.

"Thanks to your boyfriend, we have enough to convict them. And it's an ironclad case. The prosecutor's office decided to go ahead with it and issued the warrants last night."

"I don't understand? What's Greg got to do with this?"

"Mr. Lewis has been working with the district attorney's office, doing some… how shall I say it… undercover work. We asked him to remain employed at Meadowbrook Country Club, being that he had a connection with one of the suspects. As a result, he was able to get a copy of a video."

"There's a video?" Bryan's heart sank. He began to shake his head, then buried his face in his hands."

Greg immediately wrapped his arm around him. "It's okay," Greg said.

"It's not okay! I… uh… I can't believe you saw…."

"I saw what evil, sadistic bastards they are, and now all three of them are going away for a long time. Bryan, you did nothing wrong. You've nothing to be ashamed of."

"But how many people saw this video?"

"Unfortunately, it was posted on an adult website," the officer said, "but it's been removed."

"Oh God!" Bryan exclaimed. "How could they do that? How could they make a video of that and post it?"

"Bryan, we're sorry about the video," the officer said, "but because of it, we are going to convict. There is no question this was a rape."

Bryan looked over at Jeff and Brett, wondering if they'd seen this video. Jeff offered a wan smile. "Bryan, we haven't seen the video and we don't want to. The website was an extreme BDSM site. It is kind of obscure. I know that's little consolation…."

"You know what?" Bryan said, suddenly feeling a burst of confidence. "Greg's right. I have nothing to be ashamed of, and this video completely vindicates me. They were stupid to film what they did and even more idiotic to post it online. And as for people seeing it, oh well. I'd have liked to have been a fly on the wall this morning, though, when they made the arrests."

Greg leaned in and kissed Bryan sweetly on the cheek. Looking at Greg, Bryan smiled. "Thank you," he whispered. Then he glanced down and noticed Greg's other hand. It was wrapped in an ACE bandage. "What happened?" Bryan asked.

"Tell you about it later," Greg said, raising his eyebrows.

"Well, I wanted to stop by and let you know where things stand. The prosecutor will be contacting you, Bryan. Actually, she'll be in touch with both of you." He looked at Bryan and Greg. "Unless they accept a plea bargain of some sort, this will go to trial and you'll both probably have to testify."

"We're ready," Greg said. "Bring it on."

When the officer left, Bryan wasn't giddy or in any way gleeful. Perhaps he should have been, but he didn't see this turn of events as cause for celebration. He was thankful justice was being served, and he was insanely proud of Greg. He couldn't believe he had doubted him.

Bryan turned to Jeff and Greg. "Thanks, you guys, for all your support throughout this ordeal. And thanks for believing me."

"We never doubted you for a second," Brett assured him.

"Of course we didn't," Jeff added.

"If you don't mind, I need to talk to Greg alone. We'll just go up to my room."

"Or you can stay right where you are," Brett said. "We have no problem giving you a little privacy."

Bryan squared his shoulders, then leaned forward slightly. "Actually, I think I'd prefer my room. We might need more than just a little privacy."

THE SECOND after the lock clicked on the bedroom door, Bryan turned and dove for him, tackling Greg onto the bed. "You sneaky bastard!" Greg made no attempt to resist, wrapping his arms around Bryan's waist as he kissed him passionately. "Why'd you go and do something like that?" Bryan managed to ask between kisses. "You had to be a fucking hero, didn't you?"

Greg rolled over, smoothly repositioning Bryan's body so that he was lying on his back, and now Greg leaned over him. Bryan looked up into his cerulean eyes and realized Greg truly was his knight in shining armor.

"I'm not a hero," Greg whispered. "You are."

Bryan reached up, using both hands, and dragged his fingertips gently across Greg's hard chest. Tracing the definition of his pecs, which were stretching the tight fabric of the silky muscle shirt, Bryan caressed him in the most worshipful way. "Oh, no. You really *are* my hero. My superhero, and this shirt should have a big red S on it."

Greg grinned as he stared down into Bryan's face. "Is this going to be a conversation, or are we going to role-play Clark and Lois again?"

Bryan took a deep breath, then leaned forward and pressed his lips against one of Greg's firm nipples, which was clearly visible through the fabric of the shirt. "Mmm. Can't we do both?"

Greg moaned as Bryan grazed his sensitive nipple with his teeth. He pulled back, then slid off Bryan and lay down on the mattress beside him. Bryan rolled onto his side so they faced each other. "Talk first," Greg whispered. "Then play." He placed his hand alongside Bryan's face, softly stroking his cheek, then carded his fingers through Bryan's chestnut hair. "I've been obsessed with this for the past few weeks. We were so close, and I wanted more than anything to tell you about it, to explain to you why I hadn't beat the fuck out of those guys."

"Greg, you couldn't. If you had, *you'd* probably be the one in jail… or the hospital or morgue. You saw how huge that Fridge guy is."

"I don't care. I would've used a fuckin' baseball bat if I had to."

"I'm glad you didn't. But I don't totally understand. Why would the police ask you to help?"

"Well, the prosecutor assigned the case to a police detective. His name's Austin."

"Yeah, I remember him. He's the really young one. The dark-haired one."

"Right. Coincidentally, I recognized him. Last year when the Pride Center was vandalized, several of the local LGBT groups met with law enforcement to discuss the incident. It created sort of a controversy because people were freaked out. They identified it as a hate crime. All this shit went down before you even moved here."

"But I think I remember hearing about it. Maybe it was Trevor who told me."

"Yeah, well, the cops assigned a liaison to the LGBT community, and it happened to be Austin. He's gay too."

Bryan smiled. "Kinda figured that."

"Well, before Austin questioned you, he talked to me. I told him everything I knew, and at the time I just kind of lost it. Had a meltdown or something. I was really freaked out, and still majorly pissed. I told Austin I was going to track those motherfuckers down and rip them apart, limb from limb. He talked me down and said he had a better idea."

"Oh my God." Tears welled in Bryan's eyes. "You were going to do that for me?"

"I wasn't really thinking straight. I was so enraged. But Austin said if we just chilled, he suspected Ian would eventually tell us everything we needed to know. He's not the type of person who can keep his mouth shut. Austin thought eventually he'd start bragging about the shit they did to you, and he wanted someone close to Ian, someone who worked with him. He asked me if I could pretend like I wanted to make up with him, be friends again."

"That's crazy."

"Yeah, that's what I said at first, but then I thought about it. Austin was right: Ian was dying to brag about everything. At first I acted like I was pissed. I let him think I was breaking up with you because you'd cheated. I got right in his face and told him he was a slut for sleeping with my boyfriend and said you both deserved each other."

"But then how did...."

"Well, it took some time. We had to work together a lot more, after you quit. And he did his best to keep his distance from me, but then eventually came and apologized, said he was sorry for that shit with my boyfriend. Said it was a one-time thing and basically blamed it all on you. He made it sound like you were the one who'd propositioned him, that you said you wanted to do a three-way with him and Ross."

"Liar."

"I know. But I went along with it and said, yeah, I'd figured out you were nothing but a whore. Oh God, you have no idea how hard it was for me to say those things."

Bryan kissed him very softly on the lips. "Go on."

"Okay, well, he then started to throw Ross under the bus. This dude, who's supposed to be his boyfriend, Ian said all kinds of shit about. He said he was breaking up with him and started dropping all kinds of hints he wanted to get back together with me. I just played along, not discouraging him."

"You didn't have to...."

"I didn't! I swear, Bryan. I didn't even so much as kiss him. I just flirted, and it drove him crazy. I said shit like I wasn't ready for a relationship yet."

"How'd you keep him from finding out we were still together? I mean, it's not like we kept our relationship a secret."

"It helped that I stayed over here so much. I'm not even sure Ian knows where you live, and when you were at my house, you didn't have your own car at the time. Basically, it took some logistics, and he had his own secrets to worry about. He was still trying to maintain the relationship with Ross but was trying to work me on the side."

"I can't believe what a player he is. So how did you finally find out about the video? And who's this witness the cop mentioned?"

"About a week ago I agreed to go over to Ian's condo. It's his parents', actually, not the one they took you to, but it's nearby. I think Ian was planning to rekindle things with me."

Bryan couldn't believe Greg would go there alone. "Weren't you afraid they might do something to you? I mean, like they'd done to me?"

"I knew it was possible, but Ross didn't want Ian to have anything to do with me, so I doubted that was likely. And this was the first chance Ian had to get me on his own. Well, when I got there, he propositioned me, like I knew he would, and I said no. I said I wanted to take things slow, and I told him I didn't like the idea of cheating when he was still with Ross.

"He started saying that he'd broken up with Ross, that they were through. He was trying to do everything he could to seduce me. Then he even suggested we watch porn together, and he showed me this website where he'd posted some amateur videos. Several of them were solo videos of him, fucking himself with a dildo and jacking off and shit. Guess he thought it'd turn me on, but I just got up and left. I said I wasn't ready."

"Oh my God, I bet he was pissed."

Greg laughed. "I think he might have thought he was chipping away at my defenses. He was trying to get me horny, and he's so full of himself, he thought I wouldn't be able to stop thinking about seeing him in those videos. Honestly, I'm not sure, but when I got home, I logged back into that site, and I found a link to another site that had some more hardcore stuff. I'll admit it, I was curious, so I watched some of the videos."

"And that's when you found the one of me?"

"Yeah. Babe, I'm sorry."

"It's okay. I'm glad you found it."

"The witness Austin talked to was a kid who saw their SUV in his neighborhood. He said he saw them chase you down the street and tackle you, then throw you in the car. He was too scared to call 911, and he didn't want to get involved."

"What about now? He's decided to testify?"

"Yeah, Austin's been talking to him for the past few weeks, and he finally decided to do it."

"This is so crazy," Bryan said. "It sounds like an episode of *CSI* or something."

Greg laughed. "Babe, it's not over yet. Unfortunately, this whole thing could go public if it goes to trial. Are you ready for that?"

Bryan thought about it for a moment. "You know, a couple months ago, I probably would've had to say no, but at this point, I think I am. Like Jeff said, I have nothing to be ashamed of, and if I don't stand up to them, they'll do it again to someone else."

"Yeah, and Austin thinks they have already. There were other videos on there, and some are even worse, believe it or not."

"How'd they think they could get away with this?"

"They got away with it by choosing openly gay victims. They figured no one would have the balls to report them because it'd always be their word against the victim's. And the attitude a lot of gay guys have is that it's a major fantasy to be gang-banged. They think the whole kidnapping thing is just bullshit. Staged."

"Right. And even in my case, I had decided to just put the whole thing behind me because there really wasn't anything I could do to prove anything. And if I'd just gone home that night and not reported it to the police, it probably would be too late to prove anything, even with the video."

"Yup. That's probably what happened with their other victims."

"Do you have any idea how much I love you?" Bryan said, placing his hand against Greg's chest.

"No, not really. You might need to remind me."

"Come here, Clark." And they kissed.

CHAPTER
— 21 —

AS THE computer screen loaded and Bryan perused the page, he gasped. "Fuck yeah!" he shouted.

Trevor stepped into the doorway of his bedroom. "Watching porn again?"

"No." Bryan laughed. "Just got my grades. Straight As."

"Cool, man. Congrats. I always knew you were a genius."

"Hey, come 'ere." Bryan spun around in the swivel chair as Trevor entered his bedroom and took a seat on the bed. "I'm gonna really miss you guys."

"It's not like you're moving to Siberia, or even Michigan or some weird place like that. You're just gonna be a few miles away."

"I know, but I've loved living here with you."

"We're gonna miss you too, but Adam and I aren't gonna be here forever either. We'll be getting our own place, and then Dad and Father will finally have their house to themselves."

Bryan laughed. "Maybe that's why they bought me that car, to try to get rid of me sooner."

"Yeah, right. You know they love you like you're one of their own kids."

"I feel like I am. It's weird because although I feel like I've lost my two real parents—my biological parents—I've gained three new, better ones. I have two dads and a mom now."

Trevor grinned. "You really like Greg's mom, huh?"

"She's awesome. We're gonna be perfect roommates, and she even taught me how to knit."

Trevor began to giggle, then cracked up. "I can't picture you knitting."

Bryan shrugged. "What the hell, why not? I can now make some really cool toaster cozies. So you know what you'll be getting for a housewarming present when you get your new place."

"It's cool Greg's so close to his mom. I'm that way with my mom too, but when she moved to Seattle with Joey, I moved in here. We might just move into their old house when we graduate. Depends on whether we can get jobs nearby. For now, we like it here with the dads."

"Yeah, Allison is gonna be a cool roommate. I just hope Greg knows what he's getting into."

"He knows."

Bryan turned in his chair to see Greg standing in the doorway. "And he loves it." He glanced around the room, perusing the stack of boxes. "You all packed and ready to go?"

Bryan stood up and closed the distance between them. He wrapped his arms around Greg's waist and kissed him. "Ready as I'll ever be. Guess we should get this show on the road. I've got the whole weekend off work to get settled into my new home."

"Now that you've got your old job back," Trevor said, "I hope the two of you don't get burned out from seeing too much of each other."

"Oh, we already thought of that," Greg replied. "I told Martin to schedule us on opposite shifts. Besides, I don't like the competition. Bryan flirts with all the customers and steals my tips."

Bryan playfully stabbed him in the side with tickling fingers. They laughed and kissed one more time before loading the car and moving Bryan's belongings into his new home.

THE PARTY was sort of a housewarming slash end-of-year celebration. Bryan was now settled into his new household with Greg and Allison, and he had his freshman year behind him. He'd never hosted a party before, but all the guests were close friends. It should be rather informal. They didn't have a pool or a really luxurious house like Jeff and Brett, but Bryan loved his new home. He loved his new family.

Jeff and Brett were the first to arrive, and Bryan greeted them at the door with fierce bear hugs. "I'm so excited," he gushed. "You're our first guests."

Jeff kissed him on the cheek and held out an envelope. "Happy housewarming." He smiled.

Bryan stepped back and tore open the envelope, then removed the greeting card inside. It bore a handwritten inscription that read:

Bryan and Greg,

Thank you for coming into our lives. As you begin your lives together, may this be just the start of many years of happiness. We love you.

Brett and Jeff

And there was a check for three thousand dollars.

Bryan's mouth dropped open. "What?"

"It's the money from your checks you gave us every week. We've been saving it for you until you got your own place."

"You guys! You're too much. How can I accept this?"

"Shut up and take it," Brett said, and then he clapped a hand on Bryan's shoulder and affectionately squeezed.

Bryan felt a wave of emotion sweep over him. "Thank you so much." He embraced them both one more time.

Trevor, Adam, Todd, and Galen arrived shortly after the dads, and Traci then made her appearance. Greg had invited Austin, the police detective he'd worked with. It ended up being a truly informal gathering, and they served hot dogs and burgers, prepared on the outdoor grill. The real highlight of the evening occurred when Bryan heard an unexpected knock on the door and excused himself from a conversation to answer it. As he pulled the door open, his mouth dropped open in astonishment.

"Evan! Noah!" He began laughing and crying and pulled them in simultaneously for a group hug. "How come I didn't know you were coming?"

"Surprise," Greg said as he stepped up behind Bryan. "I invited them."

"I can't believe you're here. This is amazing." He ushered them inside and began making introductions.

Later, after they'd all had plenty of food and a few drinks, they gathered for group photos.

"We need a couples picture," Traci said. "Come on!" She lined them up against the living room wall. "Squeeze in everyone." She snapped the picture.

It made an awesome Facebook banner when she later e-mailed a copy to Bryan.

Jeff and Brett were in the center of the photo, arm in arm. To their right stood Adam and Trevor, and behind them were Galen and Todd. Next to them, Evan and Noah were smiling proudly. And finally, on the far right stood Bryan and Greg, the two dumb jocks.

JEFF ERNO began writing in the early 1990s. Originally his work was posted on a free, amateur website, where it was eventually discovered and published. He writes gay-themed stories that span several sub-genres including young adult, m/m romance, gay fiction, BDSM, and sci-fi.

Until recently, Erno worked as a retail store manager but now writes full time. He currently resides in southern Michigan. He loves animals, particularly cats, and enjoys reading, movies, theater, country-western music, community service, political activism, and cake decorating.

Visit his website at http://www.jefferno.com.

Dumb Jock Series

http://www.dreamspinnerpress.com

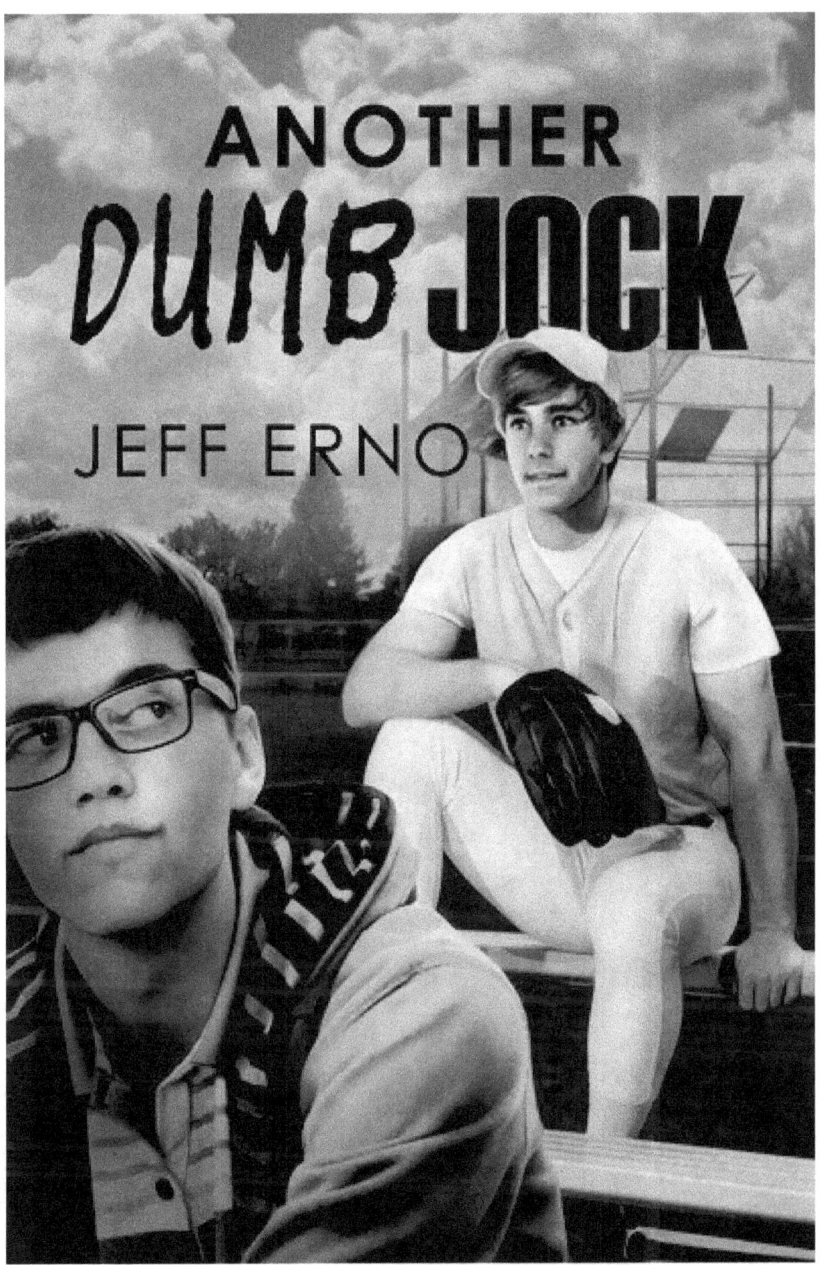

ANOTHER

DUMB JOCK

JEFF ERNO

Dumb Jock Series

APPEARANCES
MATTER
DUMB JOCK 3

JEFF ERNO

http://www.dreamspinnerpress.com

Dumb Jock Series

http://www.dreamspinnerpress.com

Also from THIS AUTHOR

Jeff Erno

http://www.dreamspinnerpress.com

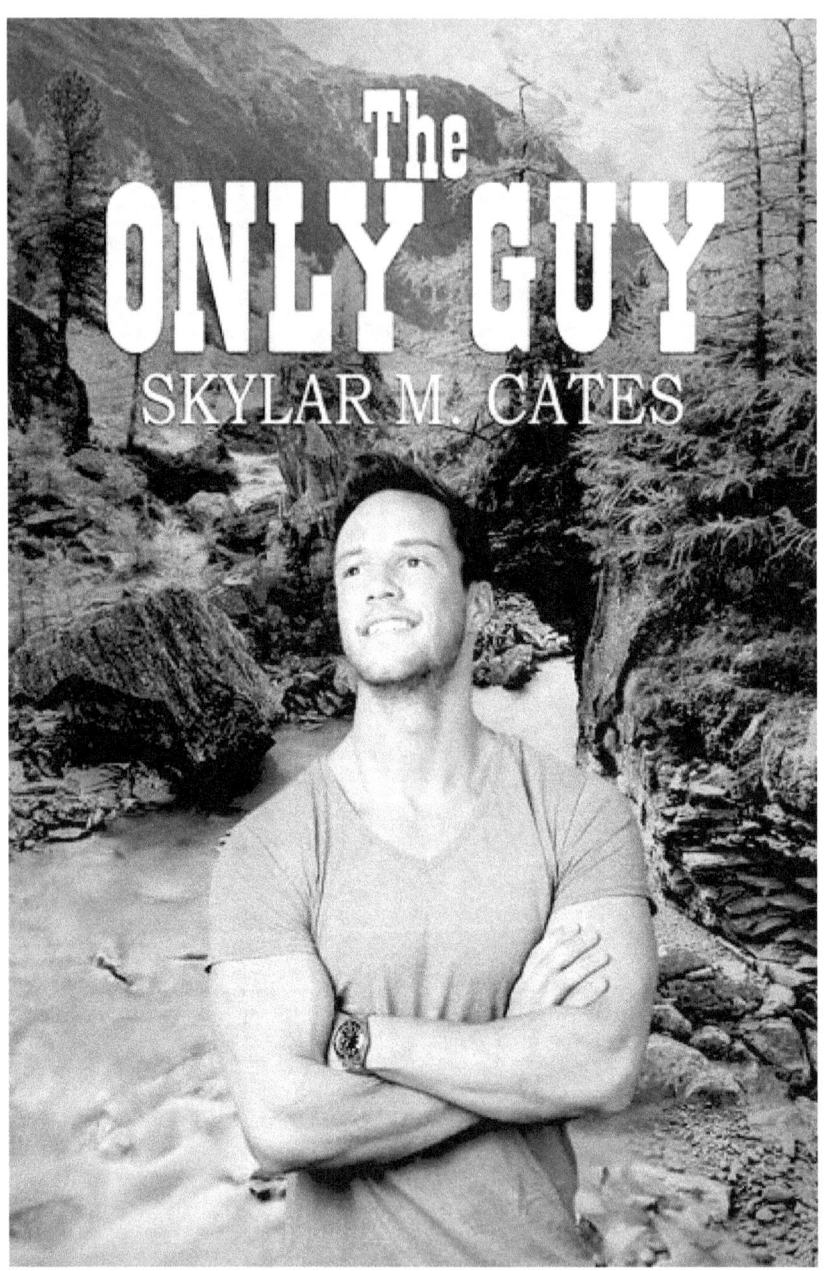

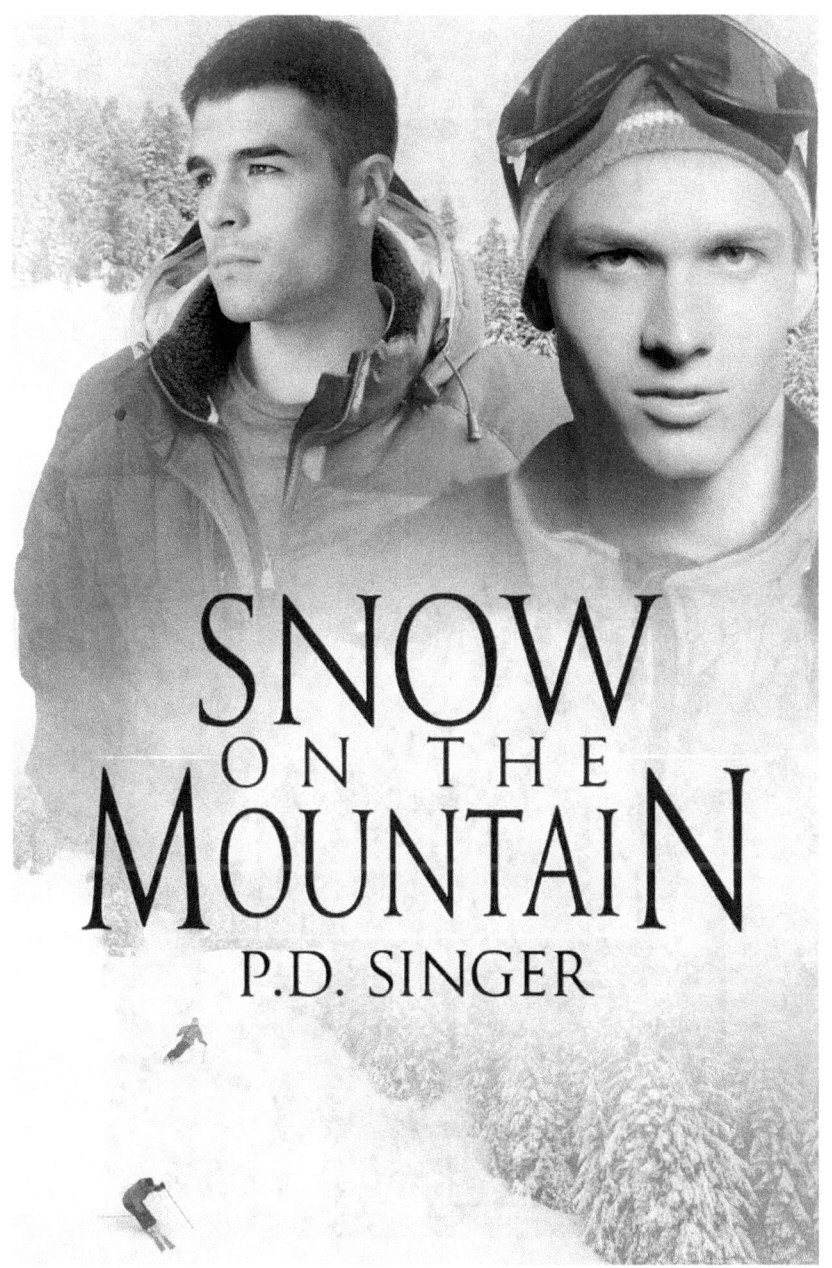

SNOW
ON THE
MOUNTAIN

P.D. SINGER

www.ingramcontent.com/pod-product-compliance
Lightning Source LLC
Chambersburg PA
CBHW070123260626
47160CB00004B/1594